Oldest Ghosts

St. Augustine Haunts

K a r e n   H a r v e y

 Pineapple Press, Inc.
Sarasota, Florida

Inquiries should be addressed to:

Pineapple Press, Inc.
P.O. Box 3889
Sarasota, Florida 34230

www.pineapplepress.com.

Library of Congress Cataloging in Publication Data

Harvey, Karen G., 1944-
    Oldest ghosts : St. Augustine haunts / Karen Harvey. – 1st ed.
        p. cm.
    Includes bibliographical references and index.
    ISBN 1-56164-222-3
        1. Ghosts—Florida—Saint Augustine. 2. Ghost stories—Florida—Saint Augustine. I. Title.

BF1472.U6 H375 2001
133.1 09759 18—dc21   00-050206

First Edition
10 9 8 7 6 5 4 3 2

Design and layout by ospreydesign
Printed in the United States of America

For Ronni

Table of Contents

Acknowledgments

I give enormous praise and thanks to my good friend Roberta "Sherlock" Butler, whose proofreading expertise expedited the writing of this book. Her friendship and zany humor made this endeavor pure fun. She also was a great organizer and listener and was always willing to make suggestions.

The guides of Tour Saint Augustine, Inc., deserve much credit for sharing their personal encounters and filling the gaps in stories about which they were more familiar.

My husband, John, and children, Kristina and Jason, deserve credit for lending support and knowing when to give me my space. The families of writers always suffer a bit, but there were no complaints, just lots of hugs as each plateau was reached.

Although my friends at the St. Augustine Historical Society will never acknowledge ghosts, we had a lot of laughs, and they were helpful in checking historical background on houses and people.

Dr. Andrew Nichols and friends Alexandra Corra and Thomas Clyde gave me insights into the world of parapsychology and the gifts of mediums. I appreciate the time and the understanding.

To "my ghosts": I hope you enjoyed the attention, and I thank you for being so cooperative and friendly. Let me know if you want more.

Introduction

Oldest Ghosts? What does that mean? Ghosts have been around for as long as people have existed on this planet. But in 1990, just a decade ago, St. Augustine's ghosts were not known by the general public.

Why not?

My theory was that residents in the nation's oldest city didn't want to talk about ghosts because paranormal activity didn't enhance the town's historic integrity. So why did I get involved with the ghosts, and why do I call them "oldest"?

First, I didn't choose to do this project. The ghosts chose me. My love of history and desire to write about this historic town made me a natural choice for them. Second, we here in St. Augustine thrive on the word "oldest." Our history as the oldest, continuously established European settlement in the continental United States is constantly questioned.

We in St. Augustine are not the oldest anything in terms of the history of the planet or certainly the universe, but we are the oldest settlement in the New World.

Much of what is happening in this town is related to its history. Our ghosts were here long before people decided to talk about them. My involvement began as the result of a phone call in 1990 to the editor of our local newspaper, the *St. Augustine Record.* I was asked why the newspaper didn't publish any ghost stories related to St. Augustine. The editor assumed I would know some ghost stories since I was knowledgeable about the history of the town. I did not know any, so the editor sent me out on assignment to find "them."

I found this assignment strange, but not a problem. I went to people living in old houses and talked to friends who also knew the history of the town and learned that there indeed were ghosts in St. Augustine. People simply had never been interviewed about them.

When I published the first of what became a series of articles about ghosts, I learned that people were eager to reveal their stories. Over a period of three years as I wrote about our ghosts, I was constantly called with new stories and learned more and more about paranormal phenomena.

While I was still working as the arts and entertainment editor for the *Record*, writer David Lapham asked me about the ghost articles. I kept photocopies of the stories in a file on my desk because requests to see them were not unusual. Lapham developed them into a book, *Ghosts of St. Augustine.* About the same time, Sandy Craig, owner of Tour Saint Augustine, Inc., added a ghost walk through the historic area of St. Augustine. The tour information was based on data developed for the public about the legends of St. Augustine's ghosts.

No one had any idea what this concept would mean to the town or to us. The first tours were run by two guides who took a handful of people around the streets, but the tour became so popular that it developed into a business with twenty certified guides. The interest in ghosts and their stories has increased, and now it is not unusual for our nightly tours to include one hundred listeners—and we have surpassed two hundred.

I became one of the guides because, I think, "they" made me do it. I was extremely reluctant to go out and tell these stories, not just because of natural stage fright, but because I really was avoiding contact with the spirits—friendly or not. Well, I agreed to join the ranks, and my worst fears were confirmed. "They" were there and "they" wanted me to tell their stories.

Do I see them? I will answer that with an emphatic "no!". So how do I know they are there? The people on my tour and on tours of other guides see them. We can explain that as the power of suggestion. But what about the times people see things before we tell the stories? And what about the people who visit a location by themselves and then ask questions about sightings they have had before meeting us?

Dave Lapham's book *Ghosts of St. Augustine* and Suzy Cain's *A Ghostly Experience* tell the ghost stories. What I have done is tell the stories behind the tales. I want everyone to know what we see and why we see it. I want to explain how the oldest ghosts relate to our history and to the spirits around the world.

If one does not believe in supernatural activity after reading these stories and related works by authorities Hans Holzer, Raymond Buckland, and others, I hope the reader will at least understand that the people sharing their stories here have witnessed another dimension of existence. Some stories come from other parts of the country. These stories were told by people who learned of the oldest ghosts of St. Augustine.

Judge Stickney, Erastus Nye, Fay, and the Bridal Ghost live on in our minds. And now they live on in the minds of those reading this book—people who may or may not be able to visit the Oldest City to experience our oldest ghosts.

Oldest
Ghosts

Chapter 1

Oldest City Sightings

Tour guide Susan Harrell stood in darkness by the wall of the historic Huguenot Cemetery. She was telling the story of Judge John B. Stickney, who paces the cemetery at night looking for gold teeth stolen when his body was exhumed in 1903.

As Susan talked, some "thing" tugged at her snood, the netlike hair covering resembling the kind women wore more than a century ago. It was playfully "pulled" by Erastus Nye, who died and was buried in the cemetery in 1835. Susan knew his name and knew he liked to tip hats and tap people on the shoulder.

How did she know who it was? "He told me," she said with a shrug indicating the obvious.

Erastus and the judge are two of several restless spirits inhabiting the cemetery and one of many walking the streets of St. Augustine, the nation's oldest city. The popular Ghost Tour takes people around the city at night and often the tourists, and sometimes the guides, have sightings or experience ghostly activity.

The story of Judge Stickney is classic. The judge, a prominent citizen of St. Augustine, came to the city after the Civil War as a widower with three children. While on a business trip to

Tour Saint Augustine guide Susan Harrell experienced numerous sightings at the Huguenot Cemetery. (Sketch by Dianne Thompson Jacoby)

Washington, D.C., in 1882, he died of typhoid fever. His body was returned to St. Augustine and buried in the Huguenot Cemetery, the Protestant burial ground opened in 1821 when Florida became a territory of the United States. After his death, his three children relocated to Washington, D.C. However, in 1903 they decided to have their father's body exhumed and shipped to Washington for a second burial. That was when the trouble began. Just as his coffin was lifted from its resting place, two inebriated men charged into the cemetery chasing the grave diggers away. They tore off the coffin lid in search of valuables buried with the judge. By the time the workers returned, the robbers had run off with all of Judge Stickney's gold teeth. Despite popular belief, they did not behead the judge to do so.

Legend has it Judge Stickney scours the graveyard at night looking for something. Conjectures include a search for his teeth, a search for the men who pulled them from his skull, and a search for a good dentist. Whatever he is looking for he certainly makes his presence known. Believed to be "the man in the tree," the judge has been spotted on several occasions as a figure in the cedar tree over his graveside monument. The tour guides are not always aware of what happened on previous tours. The "man in the tree" sighting is one that has happened during the shifts of several guides over a period of time. The scenarios are similar, with a member of the group asking, "What's that in the tree?" Then in exasperation telling the guides (who see nothing), "There is a man in the tree."

One recent sighting came during the summer of 1999 when I was showing some tourists around the cemetery. I told the Judge Stickney story, but not the part about the man in the tree. When I finished, a woman in the group queried, "Why is the judge so sad?" I was startled but responded with my own question, "Why do you ask?"

The woman said she saw Judge Stickney sitting under a tree in the middle of the cemetery. She said he was not angry (although some have said he was) but that he looked sad. Since I had not talked about his other appearances, I could only believe she really had experienced his presence.

The most recent event was the destruction of the tree limb where the judge was most often seen. During the winds of Hurricane Floyd in mid-September 1999, a large limb fell in the cemetery but did not damage any of the historic stones. Considering the size of the limb, we all were astonished at the lack of damage, a lack that we attributed to the judge and his ghostly friends.

Shortly after the limb was removed, several members of a tour group insisted they could see the judge and assured me he had simply moved up higher in the tree and was doing quite fine. The enthusiasm was enough to make me think for the first time that, yes, there was something in that tree.

Erastus Nye is another who makes his spirit presence known. The first time he expressed himself to me was when a group was filming a video at night in the Huguenot Cemetery. A psychic asked me to accompany her around the grounds. As we reached the back she stumbled and almost fell. When I asked her if she was all right she exclaimed, "It pushed me." We were standing at the grave site of three young men, all of whom had died in January 1835 and who were buried side by side with nearly identical tombstones. All had arrived in St. Augustine from northern states shortly before their early deaths. One of the three was Erastus Nye, who was thirty-five years old at the time of his demise.

Although Susan is sure it is Erastus playing pranks, Alexandra Corra, a medium who visited the cemetery recently, thinks it is John Gifford Hull, another of the trio buried there. Perhaps it is all three, the third being John Lyman. Alexandra feels that Hull died of complications of tetanus and Nye from cholera. No research has confirmed the causes of death nor the reason for all three dying in a short time period and being buried side by side. We only know they are our restless spirits. As recently as October 1999, one attractive young women confessed to having something "grab" her leg. The spirits do like to have fun.

Apparently we also have a spirit woman in the cemetery eager to be noticed. On one tour she stood beside a visitor as stories were being told. When the group prepared to move on, she simply disappeared. A tourist, not wanting to disrupt the tour, waited until the end when she confided to the guide about her encounter, fully describing the clothing worn by the spirit. She explained that she had seen someone in clothing from this century, but not of this time period. People in our groups are generally clad in shorts or jeans, depending upon the season, but this spirit woman had more of a 1950s look. I have no explanation about her appearance. I only know someone saw her.

It is reasonable to believe the cemetery has restless spirits. It opened to receive the victims of a yellow fever epidemic in 1821 shortly after Florida became a territory of the United States. The dead were buried far from family and friends and without the dignity of interment in a church-side cemetery. In fact, there were no Protestant churches in St. Augustine at that time, and the deceased could not be buried on Catholic burial grounds. Although a decade later the cemetery became the property of the Presbyterian Church, the pattern of solitary burials of transplanted Northerners continued.

At the Catholic Tolomato Cemetery on Cordova Street, sightings are so frequent that guides feel compelled to warn tourists of the possibility of seeing the unexplained light in the chapel mortuary or the figure of the Bridal Ghost. The Bridal Ghost is the name given to a woman in a long white dress. She first appeared almost a century ago to two young boys who spent the night in the cemetery. She was so real to them that they maintained their belief in seeing her throughout their long lives (they lived to be in their 80s and 90s).

Although the Bridal Ghost has been sighted in two bed and breakfast establishments near the cemetery, the experiences of guides are most intriguing. One guide who had not yet told the Bridal Ghost story was interrupted by a frightened little girl. When the guide assured her these were only stories, the little girl said, "I know but I'm frightened by that women in the white dress standing behind you."

Another guide arrived at the cemetery to find a young couple staring through the gate. She learned they were on their honeymoon, and she invited them to stay to hear the stories. They accepted the invitation but said, "What we really want to know is who the woman in the white dress is whom we saw wandering through the cemetery?"

On one occasion, I arrived to see two women clinging to the chain link gate obviously upset. I asked if I could help them, and they both nervously said they knew about the woman in white, pointing to where they had seen her. Then they said, "But who is that man in the black robe standing over there?" I had no answer for them, but felt sure I would one day find out. Less than a week later I received one of our guide updates with new information. A Franciscan missionary named Father Corpa publicly rebuked one of his Indian converts and was murdered on the cemetery grounds, which at that time was not a cemetery but an Indian village. It was he whom the women were seeing. Since then, a visitor described seeing black orbs (see glossary) in the same area.

Andrew Nichols, director of the Parapsychology Institute in Gainesville, Florida, noted that ghosts are most frequently seen in the summer and during stormy weather. Our more than twenty guides can vouch for that. During the summer of 1999, things happened that no one could explain. One evening, tour guide Lori Devouges and I took a group of fourth-graders out on a tour. We told the most frightening stories we could think of because, we believed, that was what they wanted. Toward the end of the tour I realized we were scaring the children, and we began to watch them carefully since fourth graders can be skittish as young colts, and nighttime traffic is always a safety factor in town.

We arrived at a house I personally disliked, so I asked Lori to tell the story. She stood on the stairs facing the children, and I moved behind the group. Before Lori finished, the children began to talk about seeing things. It was then I realized how scared they were. I told Lori we should move on to the Tolomato Cemetery. When we got there several children completely broke down and began crying hysterically. I said it was time to end the tour and take the children to the bus for the return trip home. The teachers immediately agreed, and we held the hands of the extremely frightened children as we walked them to the bus.

Because of the large number of tourists, several other guides were out that night. When they learned of our experience we all went back to the cemetery to try to see what might have frightened the children. By then nothing was visible, although we knew the children believed they had "seen" ghosts. Lori later told me she felt something had "pushed" her while standing on the steps of Fay's House.

As we walked through a parking lot, a street light turned off. One of the male guides laughed and said he could make it do that anytime. I walked toward my car and stopped beside the light, easily making it turn on. It is one of four lights that will flicker or turn on and off as we stand near them. The city insists that the town has no motion- or sound-sensitive lights and that there is no reason for their malfunctioning. We don't need an explanation (we know why the lights do that).

The house that frightened the children is known as Fay's House and the spirits have been as active there as at our cemeteries. Fay was a very angry and outspoken woman who did little upkeep on her house. When the stairs to the second floor deteriorated, she finally hired a carpenter to fix them. She was dissatisfied with the work and told the workman to leave. A short while later she tripped on the stairs and fell to her death. No one knew she had died until the mail carrier reported an odor coming from the house. Then the decomposing body of Fay was found.

As relatives cleaned out the house, they realized strange things were happening. Window shades were found pulled down even though they had been left up. People passing by the house said they saw a face in the window. It was, they said, the face of an angry old lady.

As our tour groups increased in size, more and more people saw Fay in the window. During one tour, a tourist took a flash shot, and at least half the group saw Fay in the window.

The tour guide who has seen Fay most frequently is Candace Fleming. After many encounters, Candace chose to tell the story from across the street rather than on the steps in front of the vacant house.

On one tour when Candace saw Fay she asked the group to raise their hand if they saw a face in the window. More than half agreed they had. On another occasion Candace followed her husband, Tim, also a tour guide, to the house and sneaked around the corner to see whether Fay would know she was there. Fay knew and popped up in the window so Candace would know the ghost couldn't be fooled.

Candace evidently has the ability to see apparitions. One sighting she recalls happened when she was a student at Flagler College, a four-year liberal arts school housed in the former Ponce de Leon Hotel. The hotel was built by Henry M. Flagler, a millionaire part-

Fay frequently appears at the dormer window of the vacant house where she died. (Photo courtesy of Jo Humphrey)

ner of John D. Rockefeller with Standard Oil Company. It opened in 1888 as a luxury hotel for the wealthy.

After Flagler's wife, Mary, died he married Mary's care giver, Ida Alice Shrouds, and honeymooned in St. Augustine. It was then that he decided to make the Ancient City a winter haven for the well-to-do. The first hotel he built was the Ponce de Leon, an elegant building that included stained-glass windows designed by Louis Comfort Tiffany, mural paintings by George W. Maynard, and ceiling canvasses by Virgilio Tojetti.

Candace was one of the first students to experience the presence of Ida Alice in the newly renovated building housing college students rather than the rich and famous. Candace and several friends were about to board an elevator when Candace saw the figure of a woman in turn-of-the-century clothing walking down the hall. The students entered the elevator but said nothing until they exited on the first floor. Candace asked, "Did you see anything up there?" With great relief they all agreed they had and described a similar vision. This was in 1970, well before we were telling and sharing ghost tales.

Since then, we have learned little by little that Mr. Flagler and Ida Alice frequently appear to the students. Some are frightened enough to leave their rooms. Others consider it fun and don't mind a bit if Mr. Flagler appears to them during the night or Ida Alice is seen pacing the halls. The security guard, Pete Cramer, laughs and says it is the imagination of college students. I am not convinced it is.

Another place of numerous sightings is a restaurant on the bayfront. At one time it was part of a chain known as Chart House. Later it was renamed Catalina's Gardens. In 1997 ownership changed again, and it became Harry's Seafood Bar and Grille. Many people believe there was less activity when it was known as Catalina's Gardens. At least one person, one of the guides on the ghost tours, feels that Catalina DePorras' presence is definitely responsible for the unusual occurrences in the house.

Catalina was the youngest of several children in a family forced to leave St. Augustine when Florida was transferred by treaty to Great Britain in 1763. While living in Cuba she dreamed of return-

Catalina's image was captured on film by passing tourist Ron Suarez. (Photo courtesy of Iron Man Ron Industries)

ing to the house she loved in St. Augustine. When after 20 years she was able to return to her town of birth, she found the home in great disrepair. She only lived there a few years before her death. It is her spirit that has recently become active. Catalina haunts the second floor ladies' restroom. She likes to throw tissues on the floor after the bathroom has been cleaned. She also "sprays" strong cologne detected even after patrons have departed and the staff is closing up. The most humorous trick is rattling the stall doors. One of the off-duty guides was in the restroom with two small children when the doors started rattling. In her words, "One of the little girls ran out before she could get her knickers up."

Another incident happened on my tour. I was telling the story of Catalina's doings when a woman said, "That happened to me today." She said she was in the stall when her purse started swinging from side to side. She was so upset she sat down in a wicker chair in the lounge to regain her composure. While there, she felt someone tap her on the shoulder and the chair move. She turned, expecting to see her luncheon companion—but no one was there.

Perhaps the most bizarre incident occurred when I saw a man in my group looking up at a third floor window. He stepped back and I could tell he was frightened. As others have done, he waited until the end of the tour to talk to me. He related he had seen a disembodied arm reaching across an unlit window. He said there was a large mitt on the hand. He was very sure of what he saw and very concerned.

I gave him my card and told him I would think about what happened and he could call me the next day. He did and I shared my theory. There have been spontaneous fires in the house that are always extinguished. The mitt he described resembled a fireman's glove. I consider it a sign that someone is keeping the fires under control.

In a humorous incident, someone saw the figure of a blond woman in the third floor window. The group thought it was a ghost, but a very real and friendly waitress took the time to come out to tell us she was a server who happened to be in the room at the time of our talk. Some ghostly appearances have very real explanations.

Some of the unexplainable stories include the St. Augustine Lighthouse and Museum, Inc. ghosts. The lighthouse and keepers' house date back to the 1870s. Much has happened at the light station during the century-plus period since it was built. In the earliest incident three young girls drowned in an accident involving a runaway rail handcar that plunged into the ocean. The victims were Mary and Eliza Pittee, the children of the Hezekiah Pittee, the superintendent for the construction of the new lighthouse, and an African American girl whose name is not known. The girls were on a handcar used to transport building materials across railroad tracks. Five girls were on the handcar when it fell into the sea. Two of the girls were rescued. Three died.

There have been numerous sightings of a young girl at the lighthouse, and she is believed to be one of these children. One incident occurred when the lighthouse was rented as a residence. A visitor went to his bedroom to retire for the night. Standing by the door was a little girl in a pale yellow dress. It badly upset him. The tenant at the time discounts all of this, but the story remains part of the legend.

The most alarming account is that of lighthouse staff member Celeste Halsema who decided to take a girlfriend to the lighthouse at night. They walked across the grassy yard between the tower and the keepers' house when the friend suddenly screamed and ran for the car. Celeste maintained her composure, walked toward the car and calmly asked what was wrong. The friend had looked up at the second floor gallery window and saw the figure of a little girl looking out at her. It frightened the young woman enough to send her running hysterically from the yard.

A little girl has been seen by many people but described differently. It is possible that both sisters appear to those who can see the spirits.

The director since 1996, Kathy Fleming, has seen the figure of a man in the basement of the keepers' house. Fleming was not the kind to get "spooked" easily, and this sighting was enough to make her depart quickly from the dark basement. The lighthouse director prior to Kathy was Cullen Chambers, who will tell you he is definitely not the type to believe in or see spirits. He has been at the Tybee Island, Georgia, lighthouse for several years. When I called him and bluntly asked if he had ever seen ghosts at the St. Augustine Light Station, he said he was completely skeptical of any-

*An 1870s photograph shows the St. Augustine Lighthouse and
keepers' house, the scene of numerous sightings.
(Photo courtesy of St. Augustine Lighthouse and Museum, Inc.)*

one who claimed to see ghosts. But, he then said, he sensed a presence in the basement of the keepers' house. He described it as the classic column of chilly air. He went on to say, "It made the hair on the back of my neck and on my arms stand up one time. From that time on I always sensed a presence."

Even with that revelation, Cullen was amazed when I told him Kathy had seen the dark figure of a man in exactly the same place and that numerous other workers did not feel comfortable going near the double cistern in the basement.

Another unusual event at the light station involves the door at the top of the tower opening during the night. The staff leaves with full assurance the tower is secured. The top of the tower is fully visible from Anastasia Boulevard, the main road on Anastasia Island passing the lighthouse. Many times in the morning the tower door will be open, although the staff knows it was closed and the tower locked when they left. The security system would show the entrance of authorized personnel, and never was there any indication of attempted entry at night. However, the door stands open. More than one staff member has seen the figure of a man on the gallery at the summit of the tower, presumably the spirit of a former keeper.

Most of the staff are not concerned about the spirits in and around the lighthouse. For decades the spirits have been there. The sound of footsteps walking up the metal stairs at night has been heard for years.

Perhaps one of the most interesting assessments of the unusual phenomena comes from Cullen Chamber's experience at the Tybee Island Lighthouse. He said, "When I first came to Tybee I opened the tower and I heard music playing at the top." He knew no one was up there but called up anyway. When there was no response he became agitated and climbed the tower to find where the music was coming from. Nobody was up there.

This is his explanation of what was happening. "As I started down I noticed the wind was blowing in such a way as to cause a breeze to come through an open window and actually react to the stairs and railing." Then he said as he walked down he could tell the wind blowing through the different windows was actually creating a harmonic quality. That was the music he was hearing.

So, some things can be explained . . . but others cannot.

No one can explain the Laundry Lady who dutifully hangs sheets and clothing in the courtyard of the Spanish Bakery on St. George Street. She appeared to four young actors who were closing a tavern late one night. Garrett Peck carried the garbage into the courtyard and saw a woman dressed in Colonial-period clothing hanging laundry over a bush and on tables and fences. He felt a typical change in temperature, but saw her as a real and solid figure.

When she did not respond to his verbal addresses he made an attempt to attract her attention visually. She still did not respond, and it was then that he noticed her clothing was blowing in a non-existent breeze.

He ran back across the street and summoned his three friends, who followed him and saw the woman still hanging up the laundry. All four said that she looked as real as any person could be and that the laundry also was real. But their actions tell a different story. No one had the nerve to touch the person they claimed was real. Then all four ran to get a fifth person without leaving anyone behind. When they returned within 45 seconds the Laundry Lady and all her laundry had disappeared. Obviously all four saw something. The fact they shared the same experience and at first sight believed the woman to be real is what makes this story unusual.

Although Garrett saw the figure only once, others have experienced the same vision. Garrett became so intrigued by the experience that during a séance, he asked the Laundry Lady's spirit why she made herself visible to him. The answer, though somewhat garbled, is as follows: "I seek you because you are a sensitive man and know many things. It is your mind it seeks. You have the answer. What is seen is my shadow. I lost a child. Can't stand the pain. Burned (or buried) to the place. You will answer me. I need to know the child lived."

The message provided more questions than answers and Garrett noted, "This isn't over yet."

Seeing solid or three-dimensional figures is unusual, considering most people think of ghosts as being transparent or shadowy. Andrew Nichols of the Parapsychology Institute at the University of Florida in Gainesville explains that most ghosts are solid, although most of the stories told here indicate they are not. As a scientist in a field that is difficult to understand empirically, Dr. Nichols is hard pressed to explain ghosts. He believes there are explanations for the things we think we see. Yet, we do see, hear, and smell the unusual.

Some things simply happen without explanation. ᴖ

C h a p t e r 2

Things That Go Bump in the Night

A t one time table-tipping and levitation were entertaining pas-times, usually hoaxes explained by unseen wires or shrewd moves by a psychic conducting a séance. But some happenings are not a ploy and cannot be easily explained.

One of these unusual events involves the moving coffin at the Horruytiner House on St. George Street. Maggie Patterson was resting one Sunday morning recovering from a minor illness. She was awakened by loud noises in the attic. Thinking it was her husband, Pat, moving furniture, she became annoyed at what she considered his inconsiderate, noisy behavior. She got out of bed just as he walked into the room and calmly explained he had returned after spending more than an hour at church across the street.

As they spoke, the noise started again. They went up to the third floor, and there in the attic was a coffin left by a doctor who had been a previous resident. They knew the coffin was there when they bought the house, but they didn't expect what they saw next. The coffin was rocking back and forth and skid marks were easily seen where the coffin had been dragged across the floor. The couple did not know who moved it or how it was moved. They only knew it happened.

Another Horruytiner House story involves the Spanish ghost. He guards the courtyard, but in recent years he has moved down the block to Pizza Hut. Yes, Pizza Hut. He either loves pizza or doesn't like having a modern chain restaurant in his historic neighborhood. Whatever the reason he tosses pots and pans around the kitchen while the staff patiently deals with this active ghost.

Jewelry and personal items are also moved around the Patterson's house. Maggie is a fastidious housekeeper with many predictable habits. She always takes her jewelry off at night and puts it back in the jewelry box. A few months after moving into the house Maggie looked for some of her rings, only to find them missing. She asked her husband whether he had moved them. Pat, of course, had not. A year later Maggie, a fanatical purse collector, was cleaning out her closet and giving away the pocketbooks not used in recent years. Maggie reached into one from the bottom of the pile. There in a pocket of the purse lay the lost rings.

A similar incident happened to Pat. A friend bequeathed him an antique ring, which Pat valued for its sentimental value but never wore. It was kept in a special box and he would occasionally look in to admire it, but he never removed it. One day he opened the box to find the ring missing. Pat was disturbed and baffled, but he was unable to solve the mystery until the night of Maggie's dream. Maggie awoke after being "told" to look in a hidden chamber behind a closet shelf. Following the directions in her dream, Maggie felt along the shelf and found a loose board. Removing it, she found a hole in the wall. Reaching in, her fingers touched a metal object. Resting in the hidden recess of the wall was the missing ring.

I had to believe these instances because a similar, bizarre thing happened to me. A few days before printing a series of articles about ghosts, I made the mistake of making fun of them in front of several people in the *St. Augustine Record* newsroom. The next day I was driving to work and noticed the ring on my finger was not the one

Spirits told Maggie Patterson where to find a missing ring.
(Sketch by Dianne Thompson Jacoby)

I had planned on wearing that day. Apparently in a hurry, I had taken this instead of another, similar gold ring from my jewelry box.

I looked at the ring I was wearing. It had been given to me by my parents years before, and I was particularly fond of the old-fashioned design, the oval onyx stone, and the tiny diamond accent.

I arrived at work during early morning darkness, parked in my usual space, and walked a typical route to my second-floor office. As I turned on the computer I noticed the onyx stone was missing. My coworkers went back with me to the parking lot, where we searched in and around my car. Frustrated, we finally gave up, but I was still convinced the stone had been in my ring as I had driven to work.

Two days later my ghost stories were printed, and I prepared for the next week's publication. That morning it was my duty to collect coffee money, a minor task done every two weeks and which involved carrying around a leather bank envelope. I opened the bag to count the money and was amazed to find the stone mixed in with the loose change. Since I only used the envelope for the two-week collection duty, I could not have lost the stone there. The friendly ghosts had forgiven me for making fun of them and had returned the onyx.

No building in the city has more things moved around in it than O. C. White's, a restaurant on the bayfront dating back to 1791. The structure was relocated stone by stone from across the street and rebuilt on its present site in the 1960s. The owner, David White, and numerous servers have experienced many odd things. At one time pots and pans departed a storage shelf, rose in the air, turned a corner, and were thrown down a staircase to the kitchen below. Not even an earthquake could have propelled them through the air in that manner.

Casey Carcaba, a teenager who has worked in the restaurant for several years, talked about an incident that happened to him. He said they used plastic cups to hold cutlery. His story: "There was one of those cups full of steak knives sitting on top of the dishwasher. I was loading some from the cup into the dishwasher. Suddenly the cup flew off the dishwasher and hit me in the back." He said another busboy was present and "bolted right out of there."

An employee who frequently opened the restaurant was still learning some of the recipes. She went in early to set up and took out the recipe notebook. The cards in plastic sleeves were used to prepare lunch. After leaving to use the restroom, she returned to find recipe cards pulled out of the plastic sleeves and scattered on the floor. (David White described the cards as so tightly inserted in the sleeves that they could not have fallen or been shaken out.) The worker replaced the recipes, walked away for a short while, and then returned to find them again on the floor.

Another time, David was closing the restaurant and was about to leave when he heard thumping in the bar area. He and another employee checked the bar and found that all the bar stools, which had previously been placed upside down on the counter, had been tipped off the bar and were lying on the floor. Curious, the two men replaced the stools and tried to lean them against each other in such a way that the process would be replicated and the stools would all tip off the counter again. Nothing the two did could make the stools fall one by one as they had before.

Two incidents in the restaurant involved necklaces. A string of pearls, lost by a customer, was found clipped around the neck of a ship's figurehead. The carved good-luck figure was used on the prow of wooden ships long ago. At one point David decided to remove the figurehead and replace it with a plaster jaguar head. This replacement coincided with the beginning of the popularity of the Jacksonville Jaguars football team. The maiden languished on the floor of the third story office while the jaguar watched over the restaurant from his prestigious spot on the wall. After several weeks the early shift entered the restaurant and were baffled by the sight they saw. Hanging from the jaguar's teeth was the sting of pearls. They had been taken from around the maiden's neck and moved to the jaguar. No one claimed responsibility, and no one was in the restaurant during the night to remove the necklace from the maiden on the third floor and place it in the jaguar's teeth.

Even more bizarre is the tale [Mrs.] Van Baker tells. Her daughter, Tory, liked to string colorful beads onto elastic string to make necklaces. She presented one to her mother as Van prepared to leave for work as hostess at O. C. White's.

The necklace was so small that Van had to roll it down over her head. She said she remembers thinking she would never be able to get it off without cutting it. She went to work, and several colleagues commented on how tight the necklace was. Van said, "It's my baby's gift, and I'm not going to take it off."

After a few hours, Van touched her throat and realized the necklace was missing. She was sure it had broken and searched the floor for the beads. She was concerned that a customer could slip and fall on one. She found no sign of the beads but knew the necklace could not have been taken from her without her feeling it.

A few hours later a coworker walked up to Van dangling the unbroken necklace from her index finger. Van was shocked and asked where she had found it. The coworker said it had been hanging from a door knob on the third floor. Van had not been to the third floor and was mystified about how the necklace could have been taken from her neck. She still gets chills thinking about the incident.

In the Foster House near the general post office a different phenomenon occurred. The house originally faced the main street, now King Street, and had one window facing the bayfront. The house was moved in the early 1900s so that it faced a different direction. The owner after the house was moved, Patti Shaw, would find pictures removed from the wall in one room. She finally discovered that the house had been turned to make way for the post office. The window that formerly faced east, looking out over the ocean, now faced a stone wall. The spirits continued to look for the window that once faced the ocean, opening curtains and moving pictures to no avail.

A tenant on the second floor of the Foster House was constantly awakened by someone knocking at her door. She worked nights and found the noise extremely annoying. Finally she told Patti Shaw about it. Patti said she had never knocked on the door when the tenant was asleep. She told the tenant to tell the person knocking to "go away." To be sure the knocking stopped, Patti went upstairs while the tenant was away and ordered the ghostly culprit to "cut it out." The knocking stopped.

Shortly after the new-found calm, the tenant would come home to find the curtains open that she had closed. She asked Patti please not to do that, and, of course, Patti said she never touched the curtains.

Patti had an antique shop on the ground floor of the Foster House. She noted that one day a roof ornament in the shop "blew straight up in the air and up the stairs." She said it was moving "full force." The ornament reached the top of the stairs and turned left.

Patti has some theories about the activity. She knows the house was built in the 1850s by Godfrey Foster, who lived there with his wife, Catherine, for about thirty years. They had a daughter, Flora, who grew up in the house.

She thinks it is Godfrey's spirit who is frustrated by the different view the house acquired after it was turned and who moves the pictures by the window. Godfrey died in 1879. She believes it is Flora who is mischievous and probably moves things such as the roof ornament. As for Catherine, Patti has heard the sound of a small person's feet scuffling around the tenant's room. She feels it is Catherine, who lived to be quite old and was rather small. It is Catherine, Patti believes, who keeps opening the curtains.

As people learn of the St. Augustine ghosts, we frequently hear similar stories. Ronni Haught writes about a very active house in San Diego, California. This is her story.

~~◆~~

San Diego, 1971: The house was old and had been a rental for some time. Before we moved into the small house in San Diego, our friends who were living there related several ghost stories [about the house] to us. The one that stands out in my mind was the one in which one night while all were sleeping, the doorknob on the front door simply fell off. This doorknob had been secure and was working with no problems when the folks had locked up for the evening.

For about two and one-half years my husband, our daughter, Karen, and I lived in the house without any noteworthy happenings. My husband's and my bedroom was always colder than the rest of the house, and we would, from time to time, hear "crashes" in there when we were in other rooms. When we would check to see what had broken, we always found that nothing had fallen. In March of 1971, we were adopted by a stray puppy. It was after Whiskers came to live with us that more strange things began to happen. The noises continued, and the room remained cool, but three specific incidents (for which neither Whiskers nor Karen was responsible) will forever remain in our memories.

The first occurred in April, when my husband and I were planning a surprise party for friends. Their daughter, who frequently babysat for us, helped us prepare the main items for her parents' surprise party the following day. Her parents called late in the evening, saying they were stopping by our house. We hid all the party things, including a heart-shaped cake not yet frosted. We put that in Karen's bedroom until after the couple left.

During the visit, Whiskers was in the room with us the entire time, and Karen, then nine years old, was sound asleep. As soon as everyone left, I went to retrieve all that had been hidden and discovered that a quarter of the cake had been cut away. No crumbs remained; it was as though that piece of the cake had never existed. The missing portion never reappeared, and another cake had to be baked.

A few weeks later my husband, just home from work, went through the house, and opened the back door to let Whiskers out. While the two were outside, the door, which was ajar, blew shut and Larry heard the skeleton key fall from the lock inside. He went inside, put the key back into the lock, and went outside, leaving the door open again. Again the door blew shut, and Larry heard the key fall again. This time the key was never found. We searched everywhere but had to go and buy another key for the door.

By this time, we were enjoying our ghost. I would talk to it although I never received a verbal response. Things continued to "fall," the bedroom remained cool as the weather warmed, and we were comfortable with our guest (or were we the guests?).

We went camping in May, and when we left, we felt that the house would be safe because our ghost would look out for us. When we returned, however, we noticed soot covered the entire kitchen as though there had been a small explosion.

We joked about our ghost's being upset because he (or she) wasn't included in the camping trip.

Upon investigation the next day, Larry discovered a burned electrical wire behind the gas stove. When the gas company's service man came, he expressed amazement that the whole house hadn't burned because we had had a gas leak and a frayed (partially burned) electric wire behind the stove. We knew why nothing awful happened!

Some time after we moved East from San Diego, Adele (our former babysitter) became acquainted with the folks who moved into our old house. They expressed to her that strange things happened frequently to them. They did not know the history of the house or know about anything experienced by previous tenants prior to talking with Adele.

The only common denominators to the three families that we can think of seem incidental: The men in each family were named Larry, and each family had a pet when incidents occurred.

I wonder where the ghost is now. ⚘

C h a p t e r   3

Contacts with the Supernatural

M any people who have numerous encounters with ghosts reach a limit to their endurance of pesky apparitions. Usually in a rash or agitated moment, they will order the entity to leave them alone. Oddly enough, it seems to work.

One of St. Augustine's best-known ghosts is Lily at the St. Francis Inn, a bed and breakfast establishment. The house dates back to 1791 when it was a private residence; it was converted to a boarding house in 1845. Several spirits inhabit the building, and the most playfully active is Lily. The story is that the nephew of one of the owners fell in love with a black slave girl. He hanged himself, realizing the futility of the romance. Lily apparently did not wish to relinquish her love and has been haunting the house since. She usually can be found in room 3-A, now called Lily's Room. Her pranks include turning lights on and off and tossing things such as women's purses on the floor.

Several years ago a woman who regularly booked the room was in the third floor hall shower when the water became hot, then turned off and on as she tried to regulate it. She finally called out, "Lily, stop this nonsense!" With that command, the water immediately returned to the normal pressure and temperature.

This guest was not the least bit afraid of Lily. In fact, she enjoyed Lily's visits with her. The shower incident, however, proved to be too frustrating, and the woman wanted to put an end to it.

A story about physical contact and television station flipping was written by Linda M. LaForte after a very difficult night at the St. Francis Inn, which she spent with a friend—and Lily and her lover. The story as told by Linda follows.

⟶✦⟵

December 23, 1998, was a momentous night for my friend Robin and me. It was the night we were guests at the St. Francis Inn.

Because of a brochure sent earlier, we had chosen a third-floor room with floor-to-ceiling windows and stained glass overlooking a romantic courtyard. The unit was called Lily's Room.

When we arrived that fateful December day the front desk clerk smiled and told us rumors of ghosts on the third floor. I gave Robin a cynical sideways glance, and explained we didn't believe in that stuff.

Our room proved to be everything the brochure said it would be. In addition to the beautiful windows leading out onto a balcony, the room's elegance was enhanced by a quaint stand-alone sink and a sumptuous bed.

We quickly unpacked and headed out for a day in Florida's oldest city. When we returned, a celebration was in progress. As we sat on the balcony sipping wine, we listened to the sounds of merriment wafting up from the courtyard. Candles graced the intimate courtyard tables, and Christmas lights adorned the trees. It was a magical night.

About eleven o'clock that evening we climbed into the warm bed for some much-needed sleep. I sank into the soft pillows and drifted off easily. Sleep was, however, interrupted in the early morning hours when a young black woman entered the room carrying a bucket. She wore a long skirt, a white apron, and a kerchief around her head. She flipped on the bathroom light and proceeded to clean the bathtub. In shock, I nudged Robin and asked, "Do you see this?" Her response? "Ignore it."

As I was trying to ignore the woman cleaning the bathroom, a white man came into the room, turned on the television and sat down to watch. He wore long pants with suspenders, a white shirt, and boots. I nudged Robin a little harder this time. Again she told me to remain quiet and ignore it.

"Ignore it?" I whispered back in shock.

Just then the television went black. The woman came out of the bathroom and started to draw a message on the screen. She seemed to be trying to communicate with us! At this point I could no longer ignore it. I sat bolt upright in bed and yelled, "What is going on here!"

The ghosts—both of them—looked at me in horror, grabbed their things, and ran from the room. My heart was pounding as I fell back on the pillows and exclaimed, "That's it! Tomorrow we're getting a refund!"

We tried to get some rest, thinking the worst was over. Little did we know. Now that our playful ghosts knew we had seen them, they decided to have some fun. The man came back and started to open and close the window and night stand drawer as we trembled in disbelief. Suddenly the sheets at the foot of the bed came undone. Something (the ghosts?) grabbed both my legs and began swinging them back and forth in the air.

I could not move. I could not scream. Closing my eyes tightly I prayed earnestly that everything would stop. Fortunately, it did. As quickly as everything began, it stopped. We knew they were gone. Nevertheless, we didn't get much sleep that night.

In the morning at breakfast we told an inn hostess our story.

"What room were you in?" she asked.

"Lily's Room," we replied.

"Oh," she casually remarked. "That room is haunted." And she told us why.

It seems that Gaspar Garcia built the structure in 1791 as a private home. In 1855 Major William Hardee bought the property. Major Hardee's nephew lived in the house and fell in love with a black slave girl named Lily.

The young couple would meet on the third floor. Word leaked out about their illicit affair. Knowing that their love was forbidden, the young man jumped to his death from the third-floor window.

Well, let me tell you something. They are still meeting up there on the third floor. After hearing the hostess' story we were very glad we were only spending one night in St. Augustine. We left on December 24 with interesting stories to tell our families at Christmas.

If you had asked me on December 22, 1998, if I believed in ghosts you would have gotten a laugh and emphatic, "No." If you had asked me again the next day you would have gotten a completely different answer.

Some contacts are initiated by an earthly being. Marla Pennington became tired of seeing a male ghost on the stairs of her St. George Street Benét Store. He was a bit threatening, and she finally told him, "Look, this is my place. You can stay if you want, but leave me alone." He never appeared to her again. She doesn't see him, and he doesn't bother her. But is he still around? She will never know.

Ghosts are not only seen, but also heard. Linda Powell and Casey Carcaba, employees at O. C. White's restaurant, attest to hearing the spirits. Casey was only eighteen years old when he told me about hearing a voice calling him. He thought it was another server, but when he turned around, nobody was there. Linda heard the female ghost that walks the stairway from the second floor to the third.

Owner David White said his first experience with the spirits was on the night he was working late and heard a woman's voice. He explained, "I can't remember exactly what she said, but it freaked me out so bad I turned off the lights and said 'it's time to go home now.'"

St. Augustine resident Walter Hoveter had an interesting (and amusing) conversation with a ghost. Walter walked into Le Pavillon restaurant and saw the apparitions of two men at the bar drinking "tankards of ale—silver tankards." Walter, who was with his wife, Kathy, told her about the two men and then made eye contact with them. Walter said, "They know I have seen them." Kathy did not see the two apparitions, but accepted the fact they were there. She had learned to live with Walter's visions.

Walter and Kathy went to a table and ordered a drink. Then the two ghosts carried their tankards to his table and sat down with him. They began talking—or at least one did. One was a big man Walter described as a "swashbuckler kind of guy with a beard and boots." He said the other was a small man who never said anything. The big man introduced himself as Will Green and explained that he had died in 1802. His silent companion, Will said, had died in 1805.

Will said he was English and that he had come over on a ship. He recalled that there had been seven boats in the harbor at the time. The British Period in Florida, from 1763 to 1784, does not coincide with Will's death but this does not discount the possibility that he was here then. Possibly he returned during the second Spanish Period, lasting from 1763 to the Territorial Period of 1821.

Will told Walter that he and his friend habitually came down from upstairs and entered the bodies of men who had been drinking. The ghosts would then go home with the men and "have their way with the men's wives."

Will finished the conversation, then he and his friend left as a party of ten finished dinner and drinks and departed from their

Swashbuckler Will Green socializes at Le Pavillon.
(Sketch by Dianne Thompson Jacoby)

table. As the group of men walked by Walter's table, one stranger smiled and gestured good-bye. Was it Will Green?

Probably. Will we ever know how the evening went with the wife? Never.

Walter explains that he has seen apparitions since the 1970s and has had several out-of-body experiences. None of this bothers him, and the incident in Le Pavillon doesn't surprise him.

Some ghostly communications come from unusual sources. Someone may listen or talk to an inanimate object in order to control what a ghost does. Willie Watson, a blind woman, collects dolls.

One of the dolls is haunted by the spirit of Willie's mother. Willie says the doll, which talks when a button is pushed, will talk when not activated by the switch. This, she says, is not the issue. The issue is what the doll talks about.

More than once the doll has alerted the family to danger. When a brother was lost, the doll "talked" six or seven times, giving information about the boy. The family realized the boy was in trouble. They searched and found him and brought him home to safety.

Willie is convinced it is her mother speaking through the doll. She enjoys the idea and can certainly use the advice and help. Because Willie is blind she would not know of the dangers lurking in and around her house without the help of the talking doll.

Possibly the most unusual communication between an earthly entity and an inanimate object was between Maggie and Pat Patterson and a dishwashing machine. The Patterson house, definitely haunted, had a dishwasher that would start running without anyone turning it on. The Pattersons called in electricians and a repairman, none of whom could resolve the problem. Finally they decided to use verbal threats to end the trouble. They told the dishwasher they would pull the plug if the activity didn't stop. Anytime they encountered a problem with the machine, they would sternly remind it that they would pull the plug—and the machine would "behave."

Some people have seen apparitions and attempted to communicate with them without success. Garrett Peck and his friends saw the solid figure of the Laundry Lady in the courtyard of the Spanish Bakery on St. George Street. They all saw her and tried to communicate with her, but even hand motions in front of her face did not evoke a response. Nothing they could do would create a reaction. As far as I know, the Laundry Lady is a solid ghost who is seen by many people but who will not speak.

Another person who has attempted to communicate with a ghost but could not get the ghost to talk with her is "Casandra." Her ghost was a small child with dark, braided hair. She was playful and unthreatening. Casandra, her husband, and one of her children saw her frequently around the house, and all were delighted to have her around. Casandra decided she needed to find out who the spirit child was and tried to talk to her. The child continued to appear, but no cajoling could elicit a response from her. To this day no one knows the little girl's name, but she remains present.

Although the little girl never spoke to Casandra, she did have physical contact with her. Casandra said she was taking a nap when she felt a small body climb up from the bottom of the bed. She described the experience: "It crawled over my body all the way up to my head and lay down." Thinking it was her daughter teasing her, she opened her eyes to give the child a hug. Nobody was there.

Contact occurred at a bed and breakfast, the Casa de La Paz, on the bayfront. A young woman came to St. Augustine in the early 1900s to regain her health in the balmy climate. She met a young man who had also come to St. Augustine because of an illness. As both regained their health, they fell in love. When both were healthy enough to return home, they decided they would leave together. As the time grew closer, the young man wanted to go on one final fishing trip. His lady friend begged him not to go, but he assured her he would be fine and said when he returned they would discuss when it would be time to leave.

The woman's worst fears were realized. A typical Florida storm blew in and the young man's boat was swamped. The man drowned, and the woman was devastated. Her health deteriorated, and finally she died at the boarding house. Today she can be seen wandering the halls of the bed and breakfast carrying a small valise and can be heard asking the question, "Is it time to leave yet? Is it time to leave?"

During her happier days at the inn, the woman was known to enjoy winding up a variety of music boxes and listening to the tunes. Currently the bed and breakfast displays a collection of the old-fashioned wind-up music players. Oddly, they will play when no one has been in the room to wind them up. It is believed that the woman is reliving the good memories.

Talking to or hearing ghosts may be unusual, but it is probably the physical contact that is most disturbing. "Casandra" was not disturbed by the presence of the little girl but Linda LaForte found it terrifying. The contacts vary greatly.

Tour guide Candace Fleming was telling a story when suddenly her lantern was grabbed from her hand. She said it was tugged hard enough to "take my arm back."

Several instances of being pushed have been reported. Perhaps the worst example is the experience of Starr Gray who shared an apartment with husband David in Abbott Mansion. The couple moved into an apartment in the large, old building fully understanding it was haunted. It was built by spinster Lucy Abbott in the 1870s, the first female land developer in St. Augustine. Although it is not the house in which Lucy died, she did reside in it, and it is the most elegant of the houses she constructed for sale in North City.

Very early in their four months of residence in the house, the Grays experienced frequent knocking at the door, but when they opened it no one was there. They also heard footsteps in the hall when no one was there. A misty image of a person appeared to David first, then to Starr. The most unnerving incidences happened to Starr, who claimed she knew that the ghost, presumably Lucy, didn't like her. Several times Starr heard a voice telling her to "get out." She did and decided she would never stay alone in the apartment. The order to get out turned into physical altercations resulting in Starr's being pushed down the stairs several times. She received injuries from these falls bad enough to require a hospital visit.

The most traumatic incident, however, occurred the day David and Starr moved out. Starr leaned out the window to call to her husband and suddenly felt the force of hands pushing her out. She struggled, screaming for several minutes before being released. When David returned to the room he found a very upset wife ready to leave immediately. Their story was printed in *Fate Magazine* and in Frank Spaeth's book, *Phantom Army of the Civil War and Other Southern Ghost Stories*.

The building, still purported to be haunted, is now run as a bed and breakfast called Old Mansion Inn. Lucy Abbott and a male ghost described as dressed in sailor's clothing of the 1800s still inhabit the house and will probably knock on the door of visitors, although there have been no more reports of violence.

Another frightening incident involving physical contact happened to Joanne Maio, an Orlando resident who lived in an old house built in 1927. She said her grandfather bought the house in 1941, and members of the family have lived there since. She grew up in the house, and her children were born while she lived there. She said she inherited the house in the early '90s and moved back into it with her husband, Patrick, and their children.

She was on the upper level of a floor with many doorways connecting numerous rooms opening to a central hallway. Joanne was unpacking in one of these upstairs rooms when she suddenly felt the presence of a female watching her.

When I asked why she thought it was female, she said she could not explain exactly why, but she sensed the presence of a woman with black hair about the same height as Joanne (five feet six inches tall) and very angry. She felt the presence wanted her to leave. She said she went to the end of the room to continue unpacking when, "All of a sudden I felt it run across the room like a cannonball." She felt the force hit her, and she "was out of kilter for a few seconds." She knew she had to leave the room, but she refused to run out screaming. She admits to being terrified but would not let the "force" take control. She walked over to turn off the lights, and the "thing" hit her again. She tried to go to the stairs, and it pushed her down the hallway. She grabbed a stairway railing, but it continued to push her. She said there were two stairway landings, and she finally regained her balance on the second one.

Joanne said the entity was trying to make her leave, and she didn't consider that fair since her family had lived in the house longer than any other and they had "squatters rights."

Finally the family prayed to get rid of any evil spirits, and that seemed to work. Joanne spoke with humor about the final episode and how she ended it. She could hear the doors to the rooms in the upper hallway slamming shut. She checked and nothing had moved. She put books against the opened doors and checked again after she heard a door slam. Nothing was moved.

She said it wasn't evil, it was more a poltergeist thing. Finally, when she had had enough she went up and screamed, "Stop it! Stop it! Stop the slamming!"

It stopped, and she walked down stairs only to reach the landing and hear one last door deliberately slammed. She compared it to a little child sticking his tongue out after being punished. She said that was the last door slamming incident they had.

Although all physical contacts are startling, some are not frightening. The "third step" at O. C. White's restaurant is notorious for people feeling something brushing by them and occasionally tripping them. No one, however, has ever fallen or been hurt as in the Abbott Mansion and Orlando house stories. I was told an interesting tale by a woman who came on the ghost tour after eating at O. C. White's that afternoon. She said she was on the stairs when she felt something hug her. Was she on the third stair? She couldn't remember the exact step, but her description tells me, yes, it was.

Chapter 4
Animal Spirits

C hildren relate to animals, and I strive to indulge them by telling stories about our four-legged spirits. On St. George Street at the Benét Store (the former home of ancestors of literary talent Stephen Vincent Benét and his siblings, Laura and William) two poodles frequently visit current owner Marla Pennington. They usually appear on the steps leading up to the second floor. This doesn't seem to bother Marla as she has seen numerous ghostly figures and frequently hears the sound of children playing and singing nursery rhymes in the courtyard when no one is there.

The white poodles were hardly a problem to her as they came and went, seemingly at their own will, and would never bother customers. It did, however, come as a great surprise to Marla when a shop visitor said that her grandmother used to live in that very house and that she had had two white poodles. The dogs apparently liked the house because, even after death, they are still there. Marla doesn't talk about them much, but she certainly is aware of their presence.

The calico cat at the haunted Horruytiner House is seen often by the Pattersons, who live there. They knew they had at least one

White poodles cavort at the Benét Store
(Sketch by Dianne Thompson Jacoby)

ghost, the spirit of a seventeenth-century soldier who guarded the house from the courtyard. But they did not know or expect the Spanish ghost cat. Pat Patterson first saw the apparition. The Patterson cats stay in the kitchen, so it was a surprise to Pat when he looked from his office door into the dining room and saw a cat on the table. He was about to remove the animal and return it to the kitchen quarters when he realized they did not have a calico cat. He started to shoo the stray off the table when it jumped down and disappeared in midair. The calico cat appeared frequently, causing no trouble, so it was not a surprise to Maggie Patterson to learn that two of her grandchildren had also encountered the ghost feline. The two boys were in the kitchen with Maggie when they asked if they could go play Nintendo upstairs. Maggie told them that was fine but warned, "Don't let the cats out." They ran up the stairs and encountered a cat on the second floor landing. Fearing they had disobeyed a house rule, they ran back to the kitchen to tell Maggie they had let one of the cats out. Maggie very calmly asked them to describe what they had seen. They said it was white with orange, brown, and black spots. Maggie responded that what they had seen was Grandpa's Spanish ghost cat. How they know it is Spanish, I can't say. How they know it is a spirit is clear. It comes and goes at its own timing and will appear only when it wants to. But, then, cats are like that.

In October 1999 I told the story about the calico cat and saw two people in the tour group conversing as I spoke. When I finished they told me they had seen the cat that morning. It was in the street and looked very strange to them. They said it was of unusual proportions with a head large for a cat that size. They also said its fur was badly mangled. They were concerned about the cat and stopped to try to help it. They discovered then that they could not find the cat and looked in several places for it, but the cat had disappeared. Did they see Pat's ghost cat? Probably.

Champ is a different story, and I like this because it has a happy ending. Champ was a big, white fluffy dog, an Eskimo Spitz. His image was used as the logo for Champ's Deli, a restaurant on Aviles Street run by Bob and Diane Sims. In Champ's later years he was blind and unfortunately fell to his death from a second floor roof. This was disturbing enough, but nothing prepared Bob and Diane for what happened later. The two bought a little Pomeranian and were treating it with the same love and care accorded Champ. But peculiar things happened. The little dog began acting strangely. Bob said it looked like a large animal was grabbing him in its mouth and shaking him. The assumption was that Champ had returned from the dead and was jealously guarding his territory.

At the same time, things were being mysteriously moved in the apartment occupied by Bob and Diane. The major item was a red blouse Diane did not usually wear. It would appear on the bed after the couple left for the day, and both denied putting it there. Books they weren't reading would be found opened in unusual places, once on the bed pillow.

Bob asked me if I knew a psychic who would come to the apartment to explain what was happening to their little dog and to them.

I went with a trusted acquaintance I believed to have psychic abilities. We sat in the apartment until she felt she had learned enough. When we left, she told Bob and Diane she would contact them the next day. Once outside she confided in me that the little dog had a medical problem unrelated to paranormal activity. She also said she felt the presence of a human rather than a spirit who was moving the clothing and books.

She contacted Bob and Diane and told them to take the little dog to a specialty clinic in Gainesville, Florida. The dog was diagnosed and treated for a severe spinal problem that was causing convulsions, so he appeared to be shaken by a larger animal.

At the same time the dog was being treated, a teenager was arrested for his pranks in the apartments near Bob and Diane. Two things are important in this story. The psychic was right on target with her analysis of the human presence, and the little dog received the appropriate medical attention and was given a clean bill of health.

A story that touched me deeply involved a woman who was going on a ghost tour with me. She was staying at a bed and breakfast inn and asked me if there were any stories connected with it. I said "No." Then I remembered that once a man staying there told me about a ghost dog he had seen at the house. The woman was startled and asked me to describe the dog. When I said I believed it was a small white dog, the woman began to cry quietly. She said she had been there a year ago with her small white dog who died shortly after their visit. She was now staying at the same inn and felt sure that the dog the man had seen was the spirit of her beloved pet.

Patti Shaw encountered more than one ghost animal. At one time she heard the sound of a cat jumping off the bed of one of her tenants. When she reiterated to the tenant that cats were not allowed in the house, the young woman insisted she did not have a cat. Patti was adamant about hearing the cat, but there was no sign of an animal in the house.

In another house Patti owned, a white Pomeranian appeared to her son and to a tenant. The tenant tripped over the dog more than once, but did not mention it. When Patti's adult son was visiting, he asked when she had gotten the dog. Surprised, Patti said she didn't have a dog. But the tenant said that of course she did and that "that thing has been trying to trip me." The tenant was relieved to learn that someone else saw the ghostly dog, particularly since no dog was being kept in the house.

Animals—earthly ones—are very able to detect what we call paranormal forces. The first experience I had with this was many years ago when I was visiting an old gate house on a former plantation in New Jersey. I was told by my cousin who lived there that the house was haunted and that the ghost inhabited one of the bedrooms. He said his dog, a Weimaraner named Grendle, would not go into that room, and suggested it was not a place I would want to stay. I wasn't the least bit concerned about sleeping there (I didn't believe in ghosts) and said I'd be happy to use the room. I walked in and Grendle followed me, much to the surprise of her owners. When I got into bed, Grendle settled at my feet and stayed there throughout the night. I understood Grendle's concern, as this was a house in which furniture moved at night and the name of the young woman who died there was etched into the pane of a window. But what made it safe for the dog to sleep in the room where the young woman died? I can only guess she felt I would keep the spirits away from her. And apparently I did.

One of the most unusual animal stories is one printed in *The Ghostly Gazetteer* by Arthur Myers. A tough German shepherd, considered vicious by the police force in a town near Philadelphia, Pennsylvania, was adopted by a family moving into an old farmhouse. Something in the house completely spooked the dog. He had been purchased for protection, but he became docile and fearful to the extent he would not go to the third floor loft without someone with him. Whatever was bothering him was more than he could endure, and within a week he plunged to his death from a third floor window. One can only hope he came back to avenge the unfriendly spirit that frightened him to death.

C h a p t e r 5

Spiritualism

S t. Augustine resident and talented artist Irene Allemano encountered the spirit world while living in Mexico. She wasn't planning to become involved in the field, but she saw an ad for a course in Kirlian photography, the photographic art that shows an energy field around a real object such as a leaf. Her interest in this photography resulted in an introduction to John Lovette, a British trance medium.

Irene joined his classes and began an unusual metaphysical journey. John Lovette taught what Irene described as courses in self-development. She said they started with simple exercises designed to increase awareness of paranormal psychic ability. John always began classes with a quiet-time reading, a selection of poetry, or excerpts from inspirational works.

The students were then given exercises to increase their innate abilities. One of the early tasks was for each student to analyze the contents of a sealed paper bag for ten minutes. Irene didn't fare well with that one. She doesn't remember what was in her bag. Some students were successful, however, and Irene said she was beginning to understand the focus of the classes.

In a later class, her assignment was to focus on the man beside her. The students were told to see what they could learn about a person simply by thinking. Irene said, "I tried to pick up something, but I couldn't get anything. All I could see in my mind's eye was a collection of the paintings by the French artist Georges Rouault (1871–1958)."

She said John's instructions were, "No matter how silly you think it is, just talk about what you have sensed by thinking."

When it was her turn to speak she told the group she couldn't focus. All she could see were Rouault paintings.

In great surprise the man responded, "I have a collection of Rouault paintings, and I'm planning to write about him."

Irene finally understood. "I get it. You can pick up on something. I thought it was some big earth-shaking information that would be revealed, but it can be anything."

She understood from that experience that one can learn from the smaller visions as well as those one reads about as "earth-shaking."

The group was working well together, and after about a year John said that because their energy field had become so well coordinated they were ready to see demonstrations. He never gave demonstrations of paranormal activity for the general public, but felt this group was prepared.

He told them all to construct cardboard cones like megaphones to bring to the next gathering. The spirit guides were going to demonstrate "direct voice," which, Irene explained, was a voice coming from "the other side."

They were told to prepare the cones and line them with strips of luminous tape. They did as requested and met at the assigned time. Irene said, "We all put our cones on the floor and prepared ourselves by clearing our minds." She explained that John read meditations, and they sang. Then John entered a trance state. She said he left his body, which was then entered by his principal spirit guide, Grey Feather.

Grey Feather, speaking through John, told the group they needed more energy and that they should speak, talk, or sing. Irene explained that their energy was necessary to summon the spirits. As the energy level increased, the cones began to move in a circle around the room. They stopped in front of each member of the group, and a message was delivered.

Irene said the messages weren't particularly interesting to her—one woman received step-by-step instructions about a real estate transaction. Other members of the group received messages, and Irene was beginning to think there was no message for her, when suddenly one of the cones hovered in front of her. She heard a feeble voice thanking her. The voice said he was Bernard's brother. Bernard, Irene explained, was a friend of hers who enjoyed music, and often the two of them exchanged ideas. The voice was thanking her for helping him.

Irene said she could barely hear the words. Then, she said, "The cone just plopped down in front of me, and that was it."

Grey Feather, still speaking through John, explained to Irene that this was the entity's first attempt to communicate and that his energy level wasn't enough to sustain a high level of concentration. He told her, "This technique we use takes much practice." Irene said learning this skill was as difficult as learning to play concert music.

Irene went on to say that the spirits had a high plane of energy. She said that the spirits on the other side used focused mental energy to communicate through the power of their thoughts. One is not hearing the voices of discarnate beings—hearing such a voice is impossible because the spirits do not have a physical voice box (a larynx). What the students were hearing from the cones was sound created because ectoplasm, taken from the body of the trance medium, had been constructed as a voice inside the cone. Irene explained that ectoplasm—the vaporous, luminous substance supposed to emanate from a medium's body during a trance—is in abundance in trance mediums. Mediums are born—one cannot go to classes to learn how to become one. They are born with an abundance of ectoplasm and can also absorb the substance from people near them.

The power of the class's concentrated thought vibrated the substance, creating sound and permitting the spirit to communicate to the earthly body. Everything that happened in the classes was always explained to the group. Irene said there was no hocus pocus. Everything worked on the principles of physics or electrodynamics.

Irene discussed the power of the mind's harnessing of a substance such as ectoplasm. She described a National Geographic special she saw on a Public Broadcasting System network. One segment showed a man wired with electrodes to a toy train. The man was able to make the train start and stop merely by thinking "go" and "stop."

Irene explained that John never knew anything that happened while he was in a trance. When he returned from the trance, the class sat quietly and let him leave for his home. He may have been exhausted, but at any rate he had no desire to talk except to say, "I hope it was an interesting session."

As Irene was going into the second year of classes, John announced it was time to demonstrate materialization. To Irene this meant "ghost." John told the students what day and time the materialization would happen and that Grey Feather would select which spirits would "come in."

They all met at the appointed time, sat in a circle, and were given flashlights with red gel over the light. As with direct voice, it was necessary to keep the room dark except for a red light. John went into the trance, and through him Grey Feather explained the procedure. He said they were not seeing incorporeal beings. They were going to see another demonstration of the power of mental energy. This time ectoplasm would be used to materialize a form.

Again the class was instructed to sing to unify the energy force and increase the general energy level in the room. Grey Feather said they should talk and laugh—anything to raise the level of energy. At one point he said, "Lighten up a little bit here."

As the students talked and sang and laughed, a filmy white substance began forming in the center of the circle. Irene explained, "It was as if unseen hands were sculpting. We saw a head beginning to form. The spirits told us we should talk—the more vibrations from voices, the more energy. As the shape took on more form, we saw a head in three-quarter profile. When we saw a neck and shoulders some of us stopped talking. But then the spirits said to keep talking."

There were several materializations, and they were talking to the members of the class. Irene emphasized that these forms were not discarnate energy; rather, materializations are created from a live form that has to have existed previously. The group saw the images, which then dissolved.

The spirits told the class that they would be shown ectoplasm from John. Irene explained, "He was sitting in his chair, and suddenly this white substance—you know what a bridal veil looks like—would be all over his head and shoulders." Then the red light went out, and when it came on again, "the substance was coming down John's arms and going over his knees and down onto the floor."

After seeing the ectoplasm, the class members were instructed through the spirits to sit with their hands in their laps with palms up. The spirits said they would pass a stream of ectoplasm over the students' hands and requested that they not try to grab it.

"I felt this substance going over this one and then this one," Irene explained holding up her hands. "It was cold and slippery. It reminded me of holding a green garden snake in my hands as a child."

Irene said she didn't know how the ectoplasm moved, but it went from person to person and everyone felt it.

When the session ended, Irene said she was very tired. The spirits had warned the students that energy would be taken from them. Irene felt she had to go home and go to bed. She called the materialization a mind-boggling experience.

During the final weeks of Irene's participation in the classes, she was able to experience a demonstration of apports, or physical objects that materialize. She said this process involves knowledge of atomic structure. Referring to activity initiated by the spirits, she said, "You disassemble the atoms and reassemble them in another place."

Her first experience involved pansies. When the first session demonstrating apport ended, the floor was strewn with pansies of all colors. She said she couldn't keep quiet as John returned to his body from the trance state. She looked down and asked, "Are these for real?" She was assured they were real and took some home and kept them in water for a week.

At her final session, she asked the spirit guides if they would give her a memento. They said, "Irene, we will try." They said they could not guarantee anything, but if they could do it they would drop something in her lap. She was told not to touch it immediately because it would be hot.

In her words, "The class ended and something fell into my lap and rolled off onto the floor. I waited all of two seconds and picked up a ring in the form of a coiled serpent—the ancient symbology of the serpent goes way back to Egyptians." She noted that it was also the symbol used by the American Medical Association. She had been studying the symbolic use of the coiled serpent and found the gift extremely significant.

Despite her delight with the gift, she was concerned about one thing. Inside were the initials RJP with the date '25. She was worried that they had taken the ring from someone. She voiced her concern to the instructor, and John assured her that the spirits would never take something from someone. He said it was lost, but the spirits wouldn't say where it had come from.

During this last class the spirits also said good-bye to Irene through a letter. Paper and pencils were placed on the floor. She said, "We could hear the pencil moving. We couldn't see it, but we could hear it moving across the page. It is very hard to read because all the letters are joined together."

Difficult it is, but it can be read. The message begins by saying, "Parting with friends is temporary death as all death is." Although somewhat cryptic, the message conveys that the spirit world can communicate with us.

Irene's adventures with the spirit world did not end in Mexico. After moving to St. Augustine, she met two interesting people who had become involved with a Ouija board. They had gotten to the

*Ectoplasm covers a trance medium as pansies fall to the floor.
(Sketch by Dianne Thompson Jacoby)*

*Ectoplasm and orbs in the Huguenot Cemetery are captured on
film by Barbara Reynolds during one of the tours.
(Photo courtesy of Tour Saint Augustine, Inc.)*

point that they didn't even need the board to receive messages. One
person acted as an antenna, and the other spoke. Irene said the
energy level was so high that the table between the two vibrated.
However, to Irene, nothing could compare to her experiences with
John Lovette.

Parapsychologist Dr. Andrew Nichols is completely scientific in
his explanation of ghosts. He understands channeling, which is
when an indirect voice can come through a medium, and he understands the direct voice process as described by Irene.

Dr. Nichols is very direct, however, about explaining projections of the mind. "We can make things happen not only to us, but also to those around us just by using our own thought process." When I commented that people sometimes see things before we tell a story, he replied that the thoughts are still there even if the words have not been spoken.

In a written explanation, Dr. Nichols describes an apparition as "a hallucination perceived by the brain of the sensitive. . . . A visual experience of a phantom is often difficult to distinguish from a visual experience of a real person. In both cases our brains are presenting us with solid-looking visual images."

He also mentions electromagnetic fields and notes that hauntings can continue for centuries, depending upon the energetic qualities of the location and the emotional charge of the original event.

Alexandra Corra, a medium, along with her friend Thomas Clyde, visited St. Augustine's haunted spots with mutual friend Roberta "Sherlock" Butler and me. We were surprised at Alexandra's belief that much of what was being seen was a thought form. She explained that people projected what they were thinking, and there were no ghosts.

I told her of the times people saw the same thing at a particular location, and she again said that most of those visions were based on the thought forms of the guides, not the appearance of a ghost.

Alex believes in past lives and at one time did past-life regressions. She now does past-life histories for those interested in knowing who they may have been in a previous life form, but she will not go into the trance state to become the person from the past.

In *The Field Guide to North American Hauntings* by W. Haden Blackman, the author writes of floating balls of light (orbs) and apparitions made of ectoplasmic mist. Photographs of trance mediums surrounded by ectoplasm can be seen in *Ghosts In Photographs* by Fred Gettings.

Is the mist seen in the Tolomato Cemetery ectoplasm? Whatever it is, many people have seen it. Carol Bradshaw related this incident. Three city policemen entered the Tolomato Cemetery responding to a call of possible vandalism. When they were halfway in they saw green slime rising from the ground. The three men exited immediately. No one will ever know what they saw, but it certainly sounds like something from a science fiction movie. ⚋⚋

C h a p t e r 6

Sounds and Smells

W e don't know who smoked cigars in the St. Augustine Lighthouse in past years, but we know someone did. Many of the employees reported the smell of cigar smoke coming from or near the base of the tower, an area now used as a museum room representing the office of the keeper and a supply room.

The most dramatic incident happened when one of the guides was leading a television film team down the steep tower stairs. She reached the base and suddenly stopped. The film crew almost bumped into her. They asked what was wrong, but she replied, "Have any of you been smoking?" When all denied smoking, she asked if they smelled the cigar smoke. They agreed they did.

The smell usually occurs in or around the base area of the lighthouse, always lingers for several minutes, and then dispels. The guides always check to see whether anyone is smoking. Using lighted tobacco products is prohibited in many areas of the light station. Although no one has ever been smoking, many of the employees have smelled the cigar smoke and probably will again.

A classic tale of a haunting smell comes from Kenneth Beeson, who as a young man worked as a tailor in Kixie's Men's Shop on St.

George Street, a store on the oldest street in the continental U.S. Kenny is part of the group we collectively call the Minorcans. They formed the core group of St. Augustine, with families coming from Minorca, Greece, Italy, and Corsica. When I contacted him he was our city mayor. He had previously been a member of the city commission and a history teacher. I did not believe he would want me to tell his story, but he didn't mind. I think he finally felt relieved to talk about what had been a terrifying situation at the time.

Although I knew temperature change and lights mysteriously turning on and off were associated with paranormal activity, I did not know the significance of smells until I heard this story.

Kenny was working at night alone in a back room of the clothing store when he first smelled a sickeningly sweet odor emanating from the two rooms adjoining the work space. The next day he asked his colleagues about the smell, and they said they did not detect anything. Kenny decided he would not discuss the problem and kept quiet about it for years, fearing people would think he was losing his mind.

Sometime after first detecting the strange smell, he started hearing the door knobs to the rooms beside his workbench turning. The doors started opening and closing. Then a signal bell started ringing, although no one was entering or exiting the building. He heard the sound of heavy footsteps on wooden floors, although there was no wood in the building. All of this happened over a long period of time, but Kenny chose not to talk about it. He told some of his close friends later but did not share the tales publicly because of his own fear and disbelief of what had happened.

As he worked one night, a friend came to keep him company. The friend was watching television when the doors suddenly opened and the room was filled with the pungent sweet odor only Kenny had smelled up to that point. The friend looked around and said, "Kenny, what is that horrible cologne you're wearing?"

Startled, Kenny said, "You can smell that?" The friend assured him he could, and Kenny said, "Let's get out of here." Kenny pulled out and activated a tape recorder he had brought to the shop. He had hoped some night to capture on tape the strange sounds he sometimes heard in the store. As his friend walked toward the door, Kenny turned to follow him and saw the image of a man's face imprinted on the back of the friend's shirt. Deciding not to frighten him, Kenny said nothing and followed him out the door.

In the morning, Kenny returned to the shop and checked the tape recorder. All the sounds he had been hearing for so long were recorded on tape—door knobs rattling, doors opening and closing, the bell ringing, and even the sound of boot-clad feet walking on a wooden floor. Alarmed but still unsure what to do, Kenny maintained silence. Before he determined how to deal with the situation, his friend died of a heart attack.

A few days later, Kenny attended the funeral of his friend. As Kenny entered the church he was overcome by the same strong odor that had plagued him over the years. It was the smell of funeral flowers. At last Kenny realized that the smell had been the premonition of his friend's death. As Kenny looked around the church, he saw the man whose image had appeared on the back of his friend's shirt. Upon inquiry, Kenny discovered that the man was the friend's brother, whom he had never seen.

At last Kenny decided it was time to take action. He talked to the parish priest, who reluctantly agreed to come and perform an exorcism service. He had never given this service before, but he saw how upset Kenny was and so agreed to try to rid the shop of the spirits.

Apparently the exorcism worked because the sounds stopped. But the smell of the funeral flowers lingered on for years. Kenny played the tape for several people, but when I asked where the tape was, Kenny said, "Oh, it (the tape) disappeared." During my research on paranormal activity I learned it is possible to record spirit-induced sounds, but it seems they can fade from the tape, which is possibly what happened to Kenny's recording.

For years I puzzled over the sound of heavy footsteps on wood. I could not understand how that related to the shop. Finally I recalled that a wooden dragoon barracks had once stood near the back of the building. I concluded it was the sound of soldiers' boots walking across the wooden floors of the barracks. That doesn't explain why Kenny was hearing the sound, but it is a possible explanation of what he heard.

Willie Watson heard sounds of a different sort. In her community of Wildwood a few miles south of St. Augustine, there is an old barn nestled under old oak trees that shade the building. Willie said that in 1954 a man and his wife lived in a house near the barn. Once late at night they heard the sound of a horse's hooves running across their property. The husband left the house with a flashlight to find and capture the horse. He followed the sounds, but they stopped as soon as he crossed the property line. The man returned and walked around the house and then toward the barn looking for tracks to determine the direction the horse had taken. No tracks were found.

In a separate incident on the same property, a family in a trailer home heard opera music coming from a nearby house and believed the neighbors were playing the radio loudly. Later, the neighbors denied playing the music, saying they were asleep when the trailer residents heard the music. The opera singing continued periodically for some time, attracting visitors to come to the area at night just to hear the music. No source of the musical presentation was ever found.

Music has also been heard at a house on Vilano Beach, an oceanfront neighborhood with several elegant homes. Three siblings, a brother and two sisters, relocated from the north and moved into a large house where they did frequent entertaining. Neighbors saw lights and heard music constantly during the partying.

On one occasion, the guests arrived and realized that the brother, Todd, was not present. On another occasion guests were surprised to be greeted by the brother but only one sister. As she welcomed them, she said her sister was away. Several weeks later, with music, lights, and laughter still coming from the house, the neighbors realized they had not seen any of the siblings for quite some time.

Concerned, the neighbors went to check on the brother and sisters. When no one answered the door, the police were contacted. As they entered the house and searched the rooms, they discovered

Music from a harpsichord is frequently heard in an old Victorian house.
(Sketch by Dianne Thompson Jacoby)

the bodies of the three siblings dressed in night clothing dead in their beds. Each body was in a different state of decomposition, but there were no signs of injury.

The bodies were removed. Autopsies yielded no answers to the causes of death, and foul play was ruled out. Although the three owners were now dead, neighbors still heard music coming from the house late at night. They continued to hear the partying until the house was finally demolished.

Unexplained music also emanated from the attic of a large old house on the southern end of St. George Street. Built in the late 1800s, the house is an architectural treasure in a unique octagonal shape with Victorian ornamentation. The building was turned into apartments in the 1950s.

Tenant Bobbi Bay reported hearing music coming from the unoccupied attic late at night. She described the music as sounding like a harpsichord but assumed it was coming from someone else's apartment. When the other tenants denied playing music, Bobbi decided she would catch the culprit in the act. The next time she heard the music she followed the sounds to a room that had been the former ballroom. She was startled to see an auburn-haired woman dressed in a yellow satin gown. She said she knew it was a ghost, but it looked real to her.

Bobbi later heard the story that this woman was the wife of a sea captain. She had occupied her time when he was away by playing a harpsichord in the attic. It was said that she died there in the attic near the beloved instrument. While there was nothing to substantiate that claim, Bobbi stood by her story that she frequently heard the music and often saw the woman in the yellow dress.

A similar incident is mentioned by Michael Norman and Beth Scott in *Haunted America* in a section entitled "The Curious Visitors." A woman clearly heard a classical tune played on a piano or harpsichord in her home. Upon investigation, the music abruptly stopped. The woman had no musical instrument in her house.

And then there is the laughter heard in the ballroom area of the former Alcazar Hotel, now the Lightner Museum and home of City Hall business offices. It is said that when construction workers were

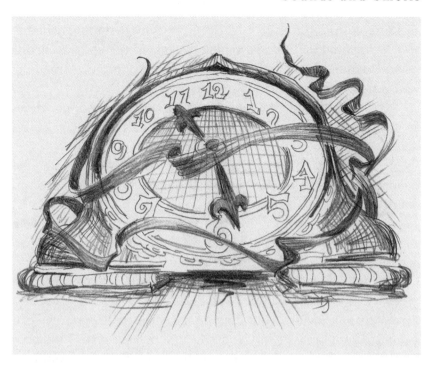

The chiming of a clock signaled a death and a tragic accident.
(Sketch by Dianne Thompson Jacoby)

doing recent renovations one stayed behind to finish a few tasks. He heard laughter and talking and thought his coworkers had returned. They had not. The cars were gone, and no one was in the building. He left immediately, vowing never to return.

The unexplained ticking or chiming of clocks can also be an indication of spiritual activity. Alonzo "Lon" Manucy reported that a clock in his grandmother's house was a pretty ornament but only worked if someone took the time to wind it. Few people did. When Lon's grandfather died the clock began chiming so loudly that the grandmother had to turn it on its side to stop the sounds. That happened in 1965. In 1973 Lon went on a hunting expedition. He was only nineteen years old, but in an unusual accident he was injured badly enough to lose his right arm. At the moment of the accident the clock started chiming again, and his grandmother knew something terrible had happened. The family did not tell her the extent of Lon's injuries for several days while they waited to see whether the arm could be saved. When the grandmother was finally informed about Lon's arm, she calmly replied she knew something had gone wrong, but she did not know what.

Lon adjusted well after the accident and never forgot the chiming clock that alerted his grandmother to the pain and agony he was suffering.

Vera Kramer at the former Abbott Mansion, now the Old Mansion Inn, has not only dealt with people being pushed down stairs but also with malfunctioning clocks. She said the clocks with pendulums often stopped and started for no apparent reason. She has had to push the pendulums to get them started. Only the battery-run clocks have never missed a tick.

Hans Holzer writes about clocks in his book *Yankee Ghosts*. In one story, a woman from New Hampshire became a companion to an elderly invalid lady. The ailing woman vacated the room she had occupied with her husband for decades. When she closed the room she left behind a large grandfather clock that was never again operational. While the companion was sleeping one night she awakened to the sound of a man's footsteps—presumably those of the elderly lady's late husband—and then heard the clock ticking with a loud sound she could almost feel. She checked the house, and the only clock that could have been making the sound was the one in the vacant bedroom not touched for years. The terrified young woman did not stay long in the house.

Another story told by Holzer relates to a clock stopping and starting with no one near it. It is believed it chimed at the time of death of a member of the family.

In the spirit realm, the chiming or ticking of clocks has nothing to do with electrical power surges. Some unexplained force makes the clocks function. ❧

Chapter 7
Unexplained Fires

Fires are frequently associated with ghosts. In *The Field Guide to North American Haunting* by W. Haden Blackman, the author explains that haunted houses may appear to be in good condition prior to the hauntings, but he lists several things that happen as it undergoes cosmetic changes. He lists mysterious fires along with bursting pipes and hot and cold spots.

Among the many books written by ghost hunter Hans Holzer, *Where the Ghosts Are* focuses on historically significant houses or otherwise well-known homes. In Fort McNair, near Washington, D.C., he writes of a house on the grounds of a former Civil War–era penitentiary. Two buildings are involved; one was the house where Mary Surratt, the woman accused of conspiracy in the Abraham Lincoln murder and hanged for the alleged crime, was imprisoned. The sounds of crying can be heard there. In the adjacent house unexplained fires erupted during the 1960s. Many historians believe Mary was innocent of the crime for which she was hanged. Perhaps she has been trying to get attention from the living.

St. Augustine has its own fire stories associated with ghosts. Lynn Cumiskey was working in a bayfront restaurant when suddenly a laundry hamper of tablecloths and uniforms began to smolder. There were no cigarettes or matches nearby and no explanation could be found for the fire. Lynn and her coworkers were extremely frightened. The incident inspired further research uncovering reports of spontaneous fires occurring in the restaurant at night. All the other fires started in the fireplaces. Occasionally candles have been found burning at night when no one was there to light them, but none of the fires or candles have damaged the building.

The house, a very old building dating back to the early 1700s, was occupied by a Spanish family with the last name of de Porras. One of their several children was a daughter named Catalina. When the family was forced to leave during the twenty-year period of British occupation of Florida, Catalina's dream was to return to the house of her childhood. She and her family finally did come back in 1784. The British had left the house in great disrepair, and paperwork for repossession was overwhelming; however, Catalina was able to realize her dream and did finally move into her beloved home, but only for six years before she died.

Catalina's spirit is believed to be one of several that haunt the house, and the stories of fires continue. In 1887 the house was destroyed by a downtown fire. Rebuilt to its original look, it survived fires in 1914 and 1926.

During one of the ghost tours a man looked up to the third floor of the house. It was evident he was upset. When the tour was over he told me he had seen a hand in the darkened window and on the hand was a large mitt. He asked me what that was or what it could mean. I told him I would think about it and call him if I had a theory explaining the image.

The next day I realized the mitt on the hand was similar to the fire-proof gloves worn in kitchens. I concluded the hand could represent the person who continually contained the fires. Catalina? We don't know. Someone puts out the fires and takes care of the building that has been a popular restaurant for many years.

Another restaurant that has experienced a fire is O. C. White's. Owner David White will not rule out arson, but that doesn't explain one unusual occurrence. The previous owner had given

David a photo in a wooden frame of the house taken at the turn of the century.

At that time, David had already experienced odd happenings. He and other workers saw or heard a woman when no one else was in the building. They attributed it to the haunting by the Worth women who once owned the building.

The fire occurred in David's office during the night. By the time he was alerted of the disaster, everything was lost. He said, "Everything burned—even the ceiling and the walls." He said the liquor stored there exploded, and his cameras melted. It appeared that someone had rummaged through his files, but nothing, including money, was stolen.

The one thing that remained untouched was the photo of the house at the turn of the century. It was still hanging on a burned wall with no damage. It remains in David's office to this day as a reminder of the event and as a good luck charm to keep other fires away.

Probably the most terrifying fire occurred at what is now Ripley's Believe It or Not! Museum. The structure was designed in the Moorish Revival style and was the winter home of William Warden, a Standard Oil partner with John D. Rockefeller and Henry Flagler. Flagler wanted Warden to help develop St. Augustine as the "Newport of the South," drawing wealthy northerners to the quaint southern town during cold winter months.

Warden chose not to participate in the project, but built his home on prime property and constructed what was known as Castle Warden, an edifice large enough to accommodate his fourteen children. In 1941 the structure became a hotel owned by Norton Baskin and his wife, Pulitzer Prize–winning author Marjorie Kinnan Rawlings, who frequently occupied a suite on the south side of the building. A suite on the north side was often used by a friend of Marjorie's, Ruth Hopkins Pickering. In April 1944 there was a fire that took the lives of Ruth, age 49, and a Jacksonville woman, Betty Neville Richeson, a young woman in her 20s. Ruth was on the fourth floor, Betty in the room below the suite. The fire was so swift and so strong that even with both women screaming from the bedroom windows, it was impossible to rescue them. Both went to their bathrooms and covered themselves with wet towels; however, they died within minutes from smoke inhalation.

They will not be forgotten because Ripley's maintains an exhibit that explains what happened to the women.

What is more interesting is that one, or perhaps both, continue to appear at a window in the room where Ruth died. People who work in the building, and some who don't, see her at the window during the morning. Again, the stories are reported from people who have not talked to each other.

The most-often-reported sightings are in the morning when people drive on the street directly facing the building. They see the face of a woman in the window of a room now unoccupied and filled with air conditioning equipment. One of the employees in the building reported that she was coming in late for work one day and stopped at the traffic light. She looked up at the face of the woman and said, "Look, I don't have time for this. Go away!" Did she? I doubt it.

Chapter 8

Guardian Angels

O ne of the most beautiful aspects of spirituality is the idea that there are guardian angels. These spirits are comforting and protective to those around them. Although the Bridal Ghost in the Tolomato Cemetery was terrifying to the two boys who saw her decades ago, she appeared to a young girl in great need of help.

The story was told to Carol Bradshaw, a ghost tour guide for several years and the curator of the Tolomato Cemetery. The event, as Carol relates it, occurred in the late 1940s or early 1950s to a little girl She was in a moving car with her parents when suddenly her door came open and she fell out. Because her clothing was caught on the door, she was dragged down the street.

Her parents, both in the front seat, didn't immediately hear her screams, but felt the breeze from the open door. When they stopped they saw in horror what had happened to their child. The girl was unconscious with injuries to her arms and legs that left bones crushed and fractured.

The girl was brought to the hospital where she was put into a full body cast. Later she was taken to her grandparents' house to recover. The house was the same one that was next to the Tolomato

Cemetery where the Bridal Ghost had been seen and where the two young boys had fled many years before.

The young girl, who couldn't move because of the cast, was sleeping fitfully one night when, in Carol's words, "There was a light and she saw the lady in white." Years later the child, now an adult, explained to Carol that she had seen a vision that wasn't walking or floating. It was simply there. The spirit came and stayed by the girl's bedside.

The child watched the woman, who was very beautiful. After awhile the woman said to the girl, "Do not be afraid, I will be here as long as you need me." The woman in white stayed until the child was able to walk again. After she was free of her body cast and had returned to her parents' home, she revisited the room where she had lain for months in recovery. She wanted to see the kind lady she called "My Angel," but the woman in white never returned. The guardian angel was no longer needed. The woman who was cared for by the angel will never forget how the spirit helped her through a harrowing experience. The woman in white—the Bridal Ghost— touched a troubled young girl with the magic wand of calming hope, and it worked.

A guardian angel watched over the child of Marla Pennington, owner/operator of the Benét Store and Dreamweavers, in downtown St. Augustine. Marla's experiences include talking to nuisance ghosts, telling them to go away, and seeing animal ghosts. The guardian angel, however, was special.

Marla experienced the presence of the angel shortly after the birth of a child. Marla would check on the baby and see the figure of a woman standing by the crib. Marla said she was not afraid. She felt great comfort in the fact someone was watching over her child during the night.

One evening I told Marla's story to a tour group. It is unusual for members of a group to speak up in front of everyone, and I was surprised when a woman said she had experienced a guardian angel. Years before, the woman, who then had a young child, had a visit from her grandmother. The old woman came to her to say she would take care of the young child. The woman telling the story said she was born after her grandmother died, and although she had seen pictures of her grandmother, she knew little about her.

Soon after the grandmother appeared to the woman, her little daughter was diagnosed with leukemia and subsequently died. The woman realized her daughter would be in the arms of her great-grandmother, a thought that was a great comfort to the family. As the woman told this story to us, I realized from the teary-eyed expressions of many in the group that guardian angels comfort us and we should welcome them into our lives. Although I changed the mood of the discussion, I saw the impact of this woman's story on members of the group.

One of our tour guides, Candace Fleming, experienced a guardian angel saving a life. She was working in a local museum when a fellow employee was climbing a ladder to change a display. The woman began to fall off the ladder but regained her foothold and was fine. Candace said the women told her she had felt the force of arms on her back, and that was what had saved her.

Randy and Linda Bruner resided in a house on Cincinnati Avenue during the 1990s. The family knew they had a ghost in the house. Research revealed that Alaska Parre and her husband, John, were the original owners of the house built around the turn of the century for Flagler employees. The story of Alaska Parre appears in David Lapham's book, *Ghosts of St. Augustine.*

Randy Bruner, who saw the ghostly Alaska, described her as "a very attractive, older woman with long gray hair, wearing a bluish-gray garment." He explained that she floated through the rooms and up and down the stairs and often turned lights on and off and played music. She loved Vivaldi. The Bruners were never bothered by Alaska. They enjoyed her. She was a bit of a poltergeist, playing tricks and moving items and trying to be helpful when necessary.

When Linda washed dishes, someone—presumably Alaska—would pull Linda's hair back and tuck it behind her ears because Linda's hands were wet.

Her most important encounter with guardian angel Alaska was when she saved Linda from injury or possible death at the time the Bruners moved into the house. According to the account in David

Lapham's book, Linda was trying to remove carpet from the top of the stairway when the carpet suddenly broke free and Linda found herself falling. Then she felt a force catch her in midair and cradle her as she floated down, "like a feather to land softly on the landing without even a thump."

Alaska was Linda's savior—a true guardian angel.

Another guardian angel in David Lapham's book took care of little Katie, during a serious illness. Katie, who was staying with her grandmother because her mother was traveling, became very sick. As the grandmother cared for the sick child she was aware of the presence of a spirit standing by the child's bed. She sensed this was not a harmful ghost and took comfort in its appearance. Katie first became sicker and then slowly regained her health after several visits from the doctor and appropriate medication. During this time, the grandmother saw the shadowy figure of a man dressed in white sitting cross-legged on the floor of Katie's bedroom. Later she saw him standing beside the bed. Never did the grandmother say anything to Katie to indicate the presence of a spirit. Several times she heard Katie talking to someone in the bedroom. When she entered and asked Katie who she was talking to, Katie said only that she was playing with her doll.

By the time Katie's mother returned from her trip, Katie had regained her health, and the grandmother had not seen the spirit for several days. After the usual greetings, Katie casually said, "Mom, did you know I have a guardian angel?"

The grandmother was stunned, only then realizing that Katie had known all the time that the spirit had been watching over her.

The mother kissed Katie and said, "Of course, darling. I know you have a guardian angel."

"No," the grandmother thought, "you have no idea."

In 1975 the Reverend Billy Graham wrote a book about angels. One of his chapters, "Angels Are for Real," gives historical references to angelic presences. I believe the current stories bring angels into the present, and I am sure they will be here for us in the future.

In *Life After Life* by Dr. Raymond A. Moody (published in book and video format) several people talk about their experiences after being declared legally dead. Two women experienced the presence of what they described as guardian angels. On the video, one woman, Sandi Rogers, described being visited by an angel who gave her all-consuming love and kindness. Her near-death experience was the result of an attempted suicide.

Another woman, Viola Horton, was pronounced clinically dead after surgical complications. She said she was in terrible pain and wanted to "get away from it." She heard the doctors say she was dead, but then felt a presence within her. It was the presence of a guardian angel. The angel, who appeared to be a woman, told Viola that she had always been there but that Viola had never been able to hear her before.

Both Sandi and Viola and others with near-death experiences have had their lives changed, and Dr. Moody claims that all have continued with a new sense of love and compassion.

Guardian angels are indeed the sweet side to spiritual stories. ⚘

Chapter 9

Frightening Ghosts

Anyone who has lived in a house with "a gateway to hell" has to have experienced some incredible incidents. The Cumiskeys are one such family. Gail, husband Jim, and daughter Lynn lived in a small modern house, not the large Victorian type typically associated with ghosts. There was nothing about the house or the Cumiskey family that would appear to welcome ghosts. They didn't believe in ghosts, and the house wasn't a place where ghosts normally roamed.

Lynn told this story about her father when she was twenty-one years old. "Out of nowhere my Dad got this overwhelming fear, just like Amityville, and he just rushed out of the house, leaving all the doors and windows open. He didn't know what it was, but he wouldn't go back in."

After that, Lynn herself had a frightening experience. She was lying in bed ready to sleep when some "thing" sat on her bed. She said, "The sheets got tight and you could feel the weight. I looked up and no one was there. But there was an imprint, like the kind you'd leave from sitting. Something sat down there to make that imprint."

A psychic was asked to evaluate the home and find the location of the spiritual activity. The family and psychic walked into the garage that had been converted into a laundry room and workshop. The psychic stopped and looked around the room, clearly concerned. She discovered what was called a "spiritual passageway" and explained to the frightened family that spirits could pass through the opening as if they were walking through a door. The psychic could not determine how long the passageway would remain open or how large it might become.

As the psychic described the phenomenon, she felt the presence of a demonic spirit trying to pass through the opening. Her frightening suggestion that the passageway could be the gateway to hell was reason enough for the residents to find a new home.

Two sisters renting an apartment on Hope Street in the north section of St. Augustine had an experience frightening enough to force them to leave their apartment. Although they always locked the doors when they went out, they would occasionally find books inexplicably moved and crumbs from food on the kitchen table when no one had eaten there. Frequently when they were outside and about to unlock their door, they heard sounds inside, although no one was there and the dog was shut out on the porch.

One sister moved from the apartment, but the second sister stayed, attributing the strange activity to practical jokes or active imaginations. Her opinion changed when she was awakened during the night by unusual sounds.

Some "thing" had opened the porch door, letting her dog into the apartment. As she put the dog back out onto the porch, she looked up to see a hand reaching around the bedroom door. The door closed.

With her hand trembling, she opened the bedroom door. Although she had clearly seen a hand, no one was there. She, too, evacuated the apartment.

Two life-threatening accidents occurred at the keepers' house at the St. Augustine Lighthouse. The duplex, built as the residence of the lighthouse keeper and the assistant keeper, was ready for occupancy by 1876. It was used by light keepers until the 1950s and then

Fire destroyed the lighthouse keepers' house. Unexplained
accidents occurred during renovation. Photo by Karen Harvey.
(Photograph courtesy of St. Augustine Lighthouse and Museum, Inc.)

as residential housing until 1969 when it was declared surplus
property by the U.S. Government. In 1970 the house was almost
destroyed by a fire that gutted the building but left the brick walls
and some of the interior intact. By 1971 St. Johns County, the county in which St. Augustine is situated, bought the property and it is
from here the story unfolds.

For a decade the house remained a skeleton of its original
Victorian beauty. When the Junior Service League of St. Augustine
took charge of the property, massive restoration took place. It was
during this restoration period that there were several terrifying incidents. Most were reported by Jon Lienlokken, a young man working with a construction crew diligently trying to restore the burned-
out building.

On the top floor of the old building the room, formerly divided into two separate apartments, was being renovated into one large gallery. As Jon and two other workers were repairing the damage, Jon suddenly felt the presence of someone behind him. He turned and saw the figure of a man hanging by a rope around his neck from one of the ceiling beams. It frightened him, but it was, in his mind, only a hallucination. A week after the incident he was told a "visitor from the sea" committed suicide by hanging himself in the upper room of the house.

Far more frightening and considered life threatening was a ghostly attack. Jon and two other employees were working on a scaffold when an iron spike suddenly shot from the wall and hit one of the men. He was injured badly enough to be taken to the hospital. The man hit by the spike was the biggest of the three and if the spike had struck Jon or the other worker they would have been knocked off the scaffold and probably killed. There was no explanation, and still isn't, of how or why the spike flew from the wall.

When the injured man returned to the job the tension was high, but the three continued to work on the restoration. Then one more thing occurred. The men were trying to remove a tree stump. They carefully secured a chain to the stump and to the back bumper of their truck. They were inching the truck away from the stump when the chain broke and flew through the back window, almost hitting the driver in the back of his head. Again, they could find no reason for this happening—they had diligently prepared for the task and had taken all necessary safety precautions.

All three finished the required work but swore never to return to the house again. They felt their presence was unwanted by some unknown entity or entities.

A local family dealt with frightening incidents that caused one family member to carry a gun into the house to ensure security. However, if it was a ghost in the house, a gun would not have helped.

The teenage daughter was cleaning up the home of a family member who had died. They all were thrilled with the prospect of moving into the house. In disposing of the articles of the deceased relative, the daughter discovered a Ouija board and a collection of magazines about the occult. At that time the teenager, alone in the house, began hearing strange sounds described as thumping noises. She reported this to her parents, who thought it was her imagination.

Several days later the mother and daughter returned to the house to complete the cleaning tasks. The sounds began again, and the teenager's father decided to explore the house with the safety of a gun. He found nothing unusual. At that point the family asked a psychic to enter the house and tell them if something unusual was going on. The psychic agreed there was spiritual activity in the house and described a man with white hair and a beard. The mother remembered throwing away a picture of a man by that description who had been a friend of the owner of the house.

As the family and psychic departed, the father carefully turned off the lights. They returned several hours later and found all the lights brightly burning. Some stories are told that the face of the man with white hair and a beard was seen in the top floor window. That cannot be verified, but the family chose not to move into the house and will never forget the experience.

Tour guide Dianne Thompson Jacoby tells the story of a Flagler College student who saw a vision in her apartment near the Tolomato Cemetery. What she saw appeared to be human, but instead of arms it had huge tendril-like appendages reaching toward her. The vision told her to leave the apartment. The spunky student ignored the warning, which was repeated three times. Soon after she met a man who had lived in the same apartment. He confided to her that while living there he too had been approached by a demon and told to leave—he had done so.

The following story was written my friend Roberta "Sherlock" Butler, a St. Augustine resident, who vividly remembers a frightening experience from her childhood.

The image of a white-haired, bearded man appeared at the window of a vacant house. (Sketch by Dianne Thompson Jacoby)

≈✦≈

The summer I was eight, my grandparents rented a small cottage for two weeks at Copake Lake in upstate New York. My grandfather, Ernie Myers, stayed in Hudson and worked at his shoe repair shop on Warren Street. Although he would drive out several nights during the week, it meant my maternal grandmother, Catherine Myers, my aunt Esther, my cousin Kathy, and I were without transportation.

It was our habit to take adventure walks in the late morning or early afternoon to explore the areas around the lake. One afternoon, Grandma, Aunt Esther pushing Kathy in the baby carriage, and I ventured beyond the lake down a dirt road. There were many in this rural resort area, about a mile or two from the center of town.

We came to an old, large stone house set a short distance back from the road. I remember we walked up the dirt driveway edged with weeds and tall grass to the back of the house where we stood on tip-toe to look in the windows. I took my turn at a window made, I believe, of old-fashioned blown glass—I remember a waviness in its texture. As I stretched up and held onto the sill, I looked into what appeared to be the kitchen of the house. There were white, painted cabinets along the opposite wall and an old-fashioned wooden table pushed or set back near the wall of cabinets. On the stone floor was a large red puddle. Mesmerized by it, I suddenly felt weak, dizzy, sick to my stomach, and I called to my aunt and my grandmother, "There's blood on the floor! There's blood on the floor!" I was hysterical.

They both ran over and looked into the window I was pointing to and then back at me. I was retreating and crying. We hurried from the house, down the driveway, and onto the dirt road we had just walked down. The next thing I remember we were back at the cottage, and my grandmother made me lie down on one of the beds while she placed a cool washcloth on my head. She spoke quietly to me, perhaps even told me a story to calm me.

When she thought I was napping, she went outside to sit with my aunt. I heard the man who owned the cottages join them on the small patio. Either he asked about me or my grandmother initiated the conversation, but I heard her saying, "I put Bobbie (me) down for a nap. Something really frightened her today. We were on our walk, down some dirt road past the lake when we came to this old stone house. We were looking in the windows in the back, when she thought she saw blood on the floor." There was a pause, and I heard Mr. Zeky ask her to describe the house. When my grandmother told him he said, "Oh, that old place? Legend around here has it that a hundred years ago, the old man killed his wife with a knife in that house. Since I've lived here, it's been sold many times, but no one seems to stay there very long."

⚜

Alonzo and Debbie Manucy had a terrifying experience that can send chills through the most stoic nonbeliever. The young couple had been through some hard times and turned to God for strength. Before going to bed one night they watched the *700 Club*, a religious program, and read Bible scriptures.

Both were sleeping when Alonzo awoke feeling a hand around his neck. He was frightened and at first couldn't speak. Finally, he was able to say, "In the name of Jesus!" And the pressure around his neck stopped.

He nudged Debbie and told her what he experienced. They both felt the presence of demons. When nothing more happened they fell asleep. Then it was Debbie who was the victim. She felt she was being choked. She said she tried to yell but could not make a sound. It felt as though the scream was in her stomach and couldn't get past her neck. When she was able to move, she woke Alonzo and said they needed to pray. They walked around the house reciting scriptures. Alonzo remembers the verse, Exodus

12:12, dealing with the Passover: "The blood on the doorposts will be a sign to mark the houses in which you live. When I see the blood, I will pass over you and will not harm you (when I punish the Egyptians)."

When they reached the living room chanting scriptures, a lamp in the corner began to sway wildly. Debbie said it was "hitting the walls and banging back and forth." Finally it stopped, everything was quiet, and they felt peace. They no longer live in the house and have maintained a strong religious faith. The choking demon has not visited them since.

Although some ghosts are frightening, most are not. Most of the time, spirits will not harm human beings and usually are more mischievous than evil. But Debbie and Lon's story, Gail's "gateway from hell," and the Abbott Mansion's threats to two families demonstrate that there is evil in the spirit world. No matter what anyone believes about ghosts or spirits, the people who have experienced the supernatural definitely believe what happened to them was very real.

Everything written here is presumed to be as true as any ghost story can be. We here in the nation's oldest city believe in our ghosts and hope they will be as kind to us as we try to be to them. If doors slam or something taps you on the shoulder, believe it. They are there. ⚘

Glossary

Apparition - Something appearing suddenly and without an explanation. The word can be used as a substitute for "ghost" or "spirit."

Apport - A physical object that materializes; literally to "distribute" or "share" in French. The theory is that an object is brought from another dimension or disintegrated from where it previously existed and reintegrated into the séance room; many apports are hot upon arrival because of a thermic reaction encountered with the law of transmutation of energy.

Asport - A physical object that disappears from a séance room and is sent to a destination outside. Literally the word means "carry away" in French.

Channeler - One who acts as a direct voice conduit for the personalities accessed. Personalities may or may not be of those who have lived on this physical plane; usually only one personality comes through with definite directive to impart information.

Clairaudience - The ability to hear or perceive sounds not normally audible; literally "clear hearing" in French.

Clairsentience - The ability to sense in some way without actually seeing or hearing; literally "clear sensing" in French.

Clairvoyance - The ability to discern objects or people not normally present; literally "clear seeing" in French.

Discarnate - Stripped of flesh.

Discarnate Being - Another word for "ghost."

Ectoplasm - In biology the word refers to the outer layer of the cytoplasm of a cell, as distinguished from endoplasm (inside). In spiritualism it means the vaporous, luminous substance supposed to emanate from the medium's body during a trance.

Electrodynamics - Electricity in motion.
    –Also the branch of physics dealing with the phenomena of electric currents and associated magnetic forces.

Haunting(s) - Visits by apparitions or ghosts.

Incorporeal - Not consisting of matter; not having a material body or substance.

Kirlian photography - The technique, invented by and named after the Russian scientists Semyon and Valentina Kirlian, is a method of photography that uses neither light nor a camera. It converts the nonelectrical properties of an object into electrical properties that can be filmed. For the first time, it has thereby made it possible to photograph auras.

Materialization - To make a spirit appear in bodily form.

Metaphysical - A coincidence or connection of events seemingly not connected in terms of logic.

Medium - A professional or an amateur who can dissociate his or her personality.

Orb - An organized pattern of energy in the shape of a sphere or any heavenly sphere, such as the sun or the moon. It is an image of spirits captured on film in places of supernatural activity.

Paranormal - Imagining information psychically, or genuinely communicating with the psychic world.

Poltergeist – From German poltern "to make noise" and Geist "spirit." In occultism, a bothersome ghost supposedly responsible for producing strange noises and wild movements or breakage of household items. Poltergeists are also blamed for throwing stones and for setting fire to clothing and furniture. Such events are said to be sporadic, unpredictable, and often repetitive. A poltergeist's activity appears to focus on a particular member of a family, usually an adolescent. A large portion of those reported to be victimized suffer from hysteria. In many instances, the activities attributed to poltergeists have been explained as natural phenomena, e.g., the creaking of boards in an old house. When strangers are present, the unusual phenomena often cease.

Psychic - A person who is sensitive to forces beyond the physical world.

Psychic phenomena - Experiences seeming logical and well ordered in the sequence of events but different from ordinary life in that they have not yet occurred or are unknown to the recipient at the time of occurrence.

Precognition - An extension of clairvoyance; to see people or objects as they will appear in the future.

Psychometry - The supposed faculty of divining knowledge about an object or about a person connected with it through contract with the object itself.

Retrocognition - Another extension of clairvoyance; to see people or objects as they have appeared in the past.

Sciomancy - Divination by communication with the dead.

Séance - A meeting to communicate with or establish contact with the nonphysical world; from the French "session," derived from the verb to "sit."

Simulacrum - An image; a mere pretense or semblance.

Trance medium - A medium who loses consciousness and passes into the control of some external force for the transmission of communications from the dead during a séance.

Bibliography

Blackman, W. Haden. *The Field Guide to North American Hauntings*. New York: Three Rivers Press, 1998.

Broughton, Richard S., Ph.D. *Parapsychology: The Controversial Science*. New York: Ballantine Books, 1991.

Buckland, Raymond. *Doors to Other Worlds: A Practical Guide to Communicating with the Spirits*. St. Paul, MN: Llewellyn Publications, 1993.

— — —, ed. *Ghosts, Hauntings and Possessions: The Best of Hans Holzer, Book I*. St. Paul, MN: Llewellyn Publications, 1995.

Caine, Suzy. *A Ghostly Experience: Tales of Saint Augustine, Florida*. St. Augustine, FL: Self-published, 1977.

Clark, Jerome. *Unexplained: 347 Strange Sightings, Incredible Occurrences, and Puzzling Physical Phenomena*. New York: Visible Ink, 1993, 1999.

Dziemianowicz, Stefan, Martin H. Greenberg, and Robert Weinberg, eds. *100 Ghastly Little Ghost Stories*. New York: Barnes and Noble Books, 1993.

Gettings, Fred. *Ghosts in Photographs*. New York: Harmony Books, 1978.

Graham, Billy. *Angels: God's Secret Agents*. Garden City, NY: Doubleday and Company, Inc., 1975.

Harvey, Karen. "Spanish Soldier Maintains Vigil." *St. Augustine Record* (Compass section) (May 24, 1990).

———. "Phenomena Continued." *St. Augustine Record* (Compass section) (June 21, 1990).

———. "More St. Augustine Uncommon Experiences." *St. Augustine Record* (Compass section) (August 1, 1991).

———. "Eerie Sights, Sounds in Old Buildings." *St. Augustine Record* (Compass section) (October 1, 1992).

———. "Hauntings Reported in Wildwood." *St. Augustine Record* (Compass section) (April 29, 1993).

Hill, Douglas, and Pat Williams. *The Supernatural*. New York: Hawthorn Books, 1965.

Holzer, Hans. *Yankee Ghosts*. New York: Bobbs-Merrill Company, Inc., 1966.

———. *Window to the Past: Exploring History Through ESP*. New York: Doubleday, 1969.

———. *Life Beyond*. Chicago: Contemporary Books, 1994.

———. *Where the Ghosts Are*. Secaucus, NJ: Citadel Press, 1998.

I Never Believed in Ghosts Until . . . 100 Real-life Encounters. Compiled by the editors of USA Weekend. Chicago Contemporary Books, 1992.

Lapham, Dave. *Ghosts of St. Augustine.* Sarasota, FL: Pineapple Press, 1997.

Martin, Margaret Rhett. *Charleston Ghosts.* Columbia, SC: University of South Carolina Press, 1963.

Mishlove, Jeffrey. *The Roots of Consciousness: Psychic Liberation Through History, Science and Experience.* New York: Random House, 1975.

Moody, Raymond A., Ph.D. *Life After Life* (video). Cascom International, 1992.

Moore, Joyce Elson. *Haunt Hunter's Guide to Florida.* Sarasota, FL: Pineapple Press, Inc., 1998.

Myers, Arthur. *The Ghostly Gazetteer.* Chicago: Contemporary Books, 1990.

Norman, Michael, and Beth Scott. *Haunted America.* New York: Tor, 1994.

Readers Digest Books. *Ghosts and Hauntings.* New York: Reader's Digest Association, Inc., 1993.

Roberts, Norma Elizabeth, and Bruce Roberts. *Lighthouse Ghosts.* Birmingham, AL: Crane Hill, 1999.

Stewart, Louis. *Life Forces: A Contemporary Guide to the Cult and Occult.* New York: Andrews and McMeel, Inc., 1980.

Time-Life Books. *Hauntings.* New York: Barnes and Noble Books, 1989.

Index

Karen Harvey has written books and articles about St. Augustine since her arrival in the Ancient City in 1978. Her works range from a pictorial history of St. Augustine and St. Johns County, now in its sixth printing, to a historic drama about the founding of the nation's oldest city and colonization of Florida. The play, *Conquest and Colonization,* caters to school and tour groups and is produced in an outdoor theater. Ms. Harvey was the arts and entertainment editor of the *St. Augustine Record* for seven years. It was there she first met her ghosts (or they met her).

Ms. Harvey also conducts ghost tours and educational tours for Tour Saint Augustine, Inc. She lives in her favorite town with her husband, John, and children Kristina and Jason.

⚜

Illustrator **Dianne Thompson Jacoby** is an artist, actress, and art educator. A Stetson University graduate, she has exhibited artwork throughout the country. Dianne currently teaches art at Flagler College, St. Augustine, Florida. She is involved with Tour Saint Augustine, Inc., ghost tours and indulges her passions for writing and producing historic plays in addition to performing living histories.

If you enjoyed reading this book, here are some other books from Pineapple Press on related topics. For a complete catalog, write to Pineapple Press, P.O. Box 3889, Sarasota, FL 34230 or call 1-800-PINEAPL (746-3275). Or visit our website at www.pineapplepress.com.

The Best Ghost Tales of North Carolina by Terrance Zepke. The actors of North Carolina's past linger among the living in this thrilling collection of ghost tales. ISBN 1-56164-233-9 (pb)

Ghosts of St. Augustine by Dave Lapham. The unique and often turbulent history of America's oldest city is told in twenty-four spooky stories that cover four hundred years' worth of ghosts. ISBN 1-56164-123-5 (pb)

Ghosts of the Carolina Coasts by Terrance Zepke. Taken from real-life occurrences and Carolina Lowcountry lore, these thirty-two spine-tingling ghost stories take place in prominent historic structures of the region. ISBN 1-56164-175-8 (pb)

Ghosts of the Georgia Coast by Don Farrant. Crumbling slave cabins, plantation homes, ancient forts—meet the ghosts that haunt Georgia's historic places. ISBN 1-56164-265-7 (pb)

Haunted Lighthouses and How to Find Them by George C. Steitz. Learn the best places to stay, dine, shop and see as you discover lighthouse history and lore. ISBN 1-56164-268-1 (pb)

Haunt Hunter's Guide to Florida by Joyce Elson Moore. Discover the general history and "haunt" history of numerous sites around the state where ghosts reside. ISBN 1-56164-150-2 (pb)

Haunting Sunshine by Jack Powell. Explore the darker side of the Sunshine State. Tour Florida's places and history through some of its best ghost stories. ISBN 1-56164-220-7 (pb)

Mystery in the Sunshine State edited by Stuart Kaminsky. An enticing selection of Florida mystery fare from some of Florida's most notable writers. ISBN 1-56164-185-5 (pb)